Forbidden Bliss

RAMONA GRAY

Chapter One

Naomi

"Naomi, you're missing family prayer time again?" My mother's disappointed tone didn't stop me from grabbing my lunch bag and hurrying toward the front door.

"Sorry, Mom. They asked me to come in to work early this morning."

She followed me to the door as my father made a disapproving 'harrumph' from the family room.

"Naomi, your father and I have been talking, and we're not sure you should continue with this job."

I froze with my hand on the doorknob, panic fluttering like an injured bird through me. She meant my father didn't think I should work, of course. I was one hundred percent certain that my mother didn't have a single thought of her own. Not after thirty years of marriage to my father.

I pasted a smile on my face and turned to face her. "I've only been working three months."

"We know and it's really taking away from our family time. You should be looking for a husband, dear, not a career."

"I'm not looking for a career." I kept my voice pleasant and low. "I just want to help you and Dad out financially and maybe save a little for when I do get married."

Liar!

My mother glanced at the open doorway of the family room. "You're twenty-three, Naomi. You need to find your husband before -"

"Before what, Mom?" I said. "I'm not an old maid."

"I didn't say that. But you don't want to," her voice lowered, and her gaze met mine before skittering away, "lose your choice in the matter."

My blood ran cold. "Like Joy, you mean?"

"Your sister made her choice." My mother's voice turned hard. "She had plenty of time to… to turn her act around and she chose not to. Your father needed to make a difficult decision."

Anger and bitterness washed in like high tide at noon. "What he did to her wasn't right and you know that."

"Keep your voice down," she said before softening. "Naomi, that isn't going to happen to you. You're a good girl. Joy was troubled and sinful, and it's your father's duty to protect his children from the sins of the world."

"I have to go. I'm going to be late," I said.

She placed her hand on my arm and it was all I could do not to push it away. My love for her had been wrapped up in a confusing blanket of grief and anger since the moment she'd allowed my father to send Joy away.

"Naomi, just consider letting Jeremiah court you. He's a handsome, virtuous young man and he's anxious to get to know you better. Your father approves of him."

I snorted. "Handsome? Jeremiah is not a handsome man."

Her gaze dropped to my body. "You're not going to get any better than Jeremiah. Not unless you finally accept your sinful food addiction and pray to God to release you from it."

My face flushed with shame, and I smoothed my hand over my skirt. "I really need to go."

I tugged my arm free of her grip and slipped out of the house. I scurried to my car and drove away without looking back.

&⁊ ⁊&

Half an hour later, parked in the employee's parking lot of Wilson Financial Advisors Inc., I dug my small makeup bag from the very bottom of my purse. Two weeks after starting my job, I'd taken a small amount of money from my very first paycheque and splurged on some makeup. I'd never worn makeup in my life, and I had sat in the chair at the department store, feeling like an imposter while the cosmetics woman eyed my skin critically.

"You don't need very much," she finally said. "You have gorgeous skin. Did you know that?"

"Oh, uh, thank you." I'd felt an unfamiliar tingle of pride at the compliment. At least something about me was pretty.

She showed me how to apply a minimal amount of shadow and blush and slicked on a soft pink gloss to my full lips. A light layer of mascara and she pronounced me perfect before showing me my reflection in the mirror.

"Wow," I said

She grinned at me. "A little makeup can go a long way."

Now, I applied the makeup using the visor mirror. The first few days it felt awkward, and I couldn't help hearing my father's voice in my head screaming that I was a painted woman. I brushed the gloss on my bottom lip and then screamed when someone knocked on my window, smearing gloss across my chin.

"Sorry!" My co-worker Jemma's cheerful face grinned at me through the window. "I didn't mean to scare you."

My heart pounding in my chest, I quickly wiped the gloss from my chin and tossed the tube into my purse. I climbed out of my car and smiled at Jemma. "Morning."

"Hey, Naomi. How are you?"

"Good." We crossed the parking lot toward our office building. "How are you?"

"Fucking fantastic," she crowed. "I got laid this weekend."

My cheeks turned bright red and Jemma giggled. "Sorry, sweetie. I always forget the mere mention of sex makes you blush.'

"It does not," I said.

"Sure, it doesn't." She eyed me up and down.

"Is that a new skirt?"

I tugged at the waistband of my skirt. My mother had made it. She made most of our clothes and after announcing that all of my skirts were much too tight, she'd made me four new ones. These ones were even more shapeless than the other skirts and secretly, I thought they were much too big. If my mother hadn't put in an elastic waistband on the skirts, they would have fallen right off me.

I sighed inwardly. Creating bigger and more shapeless clothes was my mother's way of shaming me about my size. Short and slender, she was always slightly puzzled by my height and my weight. Never quite able to understand how someone who looked like her had given birth to someone who looked like me. I was chubby from the start and while I did enjoy my food, I always privately thought that my large bottom, wide hips, and generous breasts were more genetic than a food addiction.

"Yes," I said when I realized that Jemma was waiting for my reply.

"It's, um, nice," she said. "I like the colour."

"Thank you."

It was a boring navy blue. My father didn't allow us to wear what he termed flashy colours, and I stared longingly at Jemma's bright pink skirt. The colour was amazing, and I wondered briefly what it would be like to wear a skirt that short. It was well above her knees and I admired her tanned thighs and calves. My legs were lily-white thanks to their rare exposure to the sun.

My gaze drifted to her shirt. A shimmery silver,

it clung to her slender waist and dipped low at the neckline to show off the tops of her small breasts. In contrast, my plain white shirt was buttoned securely to the neck and as too big for me as the rest of my clothes were.

I pushed down my yearning for new clothes. Spending the money on the makeup was risky enough. I couldn't afford to use my hard-earned money to buy new clothes. I'd taken a job to save money for my escape, not luxuries. My father would sell me off like he'd sold Joy, I knew that without a doubt, and this job was my only chance of escaping my fate.

If you allowed Jeremiah to court you, it would buy you some time.

Yes, it would, but the thought of having Jeremiah court me made shivers run down my spine. It wasn't just that he was unattractive, it was his mannerisms and his tone of voice and the way he looked at me like I was his property. His similarities to my father made me shudder.

"Naomi? Earth to Naomi?"

I pushed thoughts of Jeremiah and my father out of my head and smiled at Jemma. "Sorry, what did you say?"

"Why do you put your makeup on in the car every morning?" She opened the double doors to the building and motioned for me to go ahead.

"Oh, uh, always running late," I fibbed.

If my father saw me wearing makeup, he'd have me on my knees and praying for the fate of my eternal soul for hours.

"Right," she said as we stepped into the

elevator.

Anxious to change the subject, I said, "Tell me about your new boyfriend."

"Boyfriend?" She snorted laughter. "Oh, honey, no. He's not my boyfriend. Just some random guy I hooked up with and will never see again but woo – that man's dick was something else."

My face heated again but Jemma, engrossed in explaining in detail what exactly the guy's dick had done for her, didn't notice. I listened silently, wishing feverishly that I was normal and could participate in conversations about the opposite sex.

Dane

"You know," Mason stood next to me and glanced at my crotch, "if your sweet little PA knew exactly what you wanted to do to her, she'd run screaming from the building."

I ignored him and my throbbing erection, my gaze remaining on the curvy woman in the shapeless clothes walking across the parking lot.

Mason leaned forward and stared out the window of my office. "Jesus, her clothes are even looser than normal. What is up with that?"

"She's shy," I grunted.

"So she wears ill-fitting clothes? Being shy is no excuse for bad fashion choices. I'm not even sure why you find her so damn hot."

"Like hell you don't. You want her just as much as I do, Mason."

"It's true," he admitted with a grin. "There's just something about her that makes my dick hard as a fucking rock."

He adjusted his own erection as we studied the woman together.

"You know I'm going to have to seduce her first, right? She's terrified of you," Mason said.

I glared at him before stalking back to my desk. "She isn't terrified of me."

"Are you kidding? You even glance at her and she drops her gaze to the floor and starts shaking." He continued to stare at Naomi, his hand rubbing at his cock. "We like our women to be submissive, not terrified."

"I haven't done anything to make her afraid of me," I said.

Mason walked away from the window, running one hand through his short blond hair before dropping into the chair across from my desk. "Maybe not, but you do frighten her. You could try being a little gentler with her."

"I don't do gentle," I said. "That's your department, remember? You do the sweet talking, and I do the hard fucking until they've cum so many times they can't remember their own goddamn name."

"Hey!" Mason stared at me indignantly. "I am more than capable of fucking a woman into forgetting her name."

I rolled my eyes and then checked my email. Mason sat back in the chair. "All I'm saying is that you're going to need a softer touch with Miss Naomi Morris. She's not like our usual conquests."

"Do you ever get tired of seeing them as conquests?" I said.

"You getting tired of fucking around, Dane? You want to settle down with a good woman and make babies with her?"

"No, of course not."

"Not so sure I believe you, buddy," Mason said. "There's nothing wrong with wanting to quit our whoring ways and find a woman, but," he pointed his finger at me, "Naomi Morris is not that woman. There's no way in hell she would agree to a permanent relationship with the both of us. Hell, we have our work cut out for us just getting her to agree to fuck the two of us for a weekend."

"Maybe we shouldn't even do that to her," I said moodily.

Mason blinked at me. "What? You've been lusting after her for weeks – *I've* been lusting after her for weeks – and now suddenly you want to change the plan?"

"She's not like the others," I said.

"No, she isn't," Mason said, "and that's what makes it so hot. Can you imagine what it will be like to strip off those awful clothes and finally see those curves of hers?"

I could imagine it, had been imagining it on an hourly basis for the last three months, and that was the problem. I was so hot for my shy, sweet PA, that my dick was making all the decisions.

"Dane." Mason leaned forward and tapped his finger on my desk. "You need to know that even if you decide not to do this, I still will."

"Seriously?" I was more hurt by his admission

than I wanted to admit.

"Sorry, buddy, but I want this woman as much as you do. I'm not missing out on her because you're getting cold feet about seducing someone as sweet as her. Besides, you would do the same thing if the roles were reversed. Admit it."

He was right. And my hesitancy about seducing her would end the moment she walked into my office. It always did. Her light blue eyes, dark hair, and utterly fuckable lips had started an obsession that I couldn't - didn't want to – ignore.

"So, operation 'seduce your sweet little PA' has officially started, yeah?" Mason said with a grin.

I scowled at him. "You really need to knock it off with the stupid code names."

"You love them, and you know it." Whistling, Mason strode from my office, shutting the door behind him.

Chapter Two

Naomi

"What are you doing this weekend?" Jemma said as we grabbed our morning coffee from the kitchen.

"I have church on Sunday,"

"You want to go shopping with me on Saturday?" Jemma poured a healthy dollop of cream into her coffee. "I'm going to the mall to do some birthday shopping for my mom and we could even, I don't know, check out a few clothing stores."

Her gaze slid over my ill-fitting outfit again and my cheeks flushed. I took the creamer from her. "Uh, thanks for the offer, Jemma, but I don't think -"

"Come on, Naomi," Jemma said. "I hate shopping alone."

I poured cream into my coffee and stirred it as I considered what to say. Jemma had started working for the company a month ago and despite our different lifestyles, I really liked her. I didn't have many friends – hell, I didn't have *any* friends thanks to my father's controlling attitude – and the urge to pretend to be normal, to go shopping with a friend was hard to resist. I usually spent Saturdays with my parents or participating in a church related activity.

"Can I, um, get back to you about it?" I said, as if I actually might go with her. I wanted to pretend I was normal for a little longer.

"Sure," Jemma said. "Just let me know by Friday. Okay?"

"Yeah, okay. Thanks."

We both paused when we heard the deep voice behind us. "Good morning, ladies. You're looking lovely this morning."

I turned and gave Mason Shaw, the CFO of the company, a nervous smile but Jemma's face lit up.

In a low seductive voice that I knew I would never be able to imitate, she said, "Hello, Mr. Shaw. How was your weekend?"

"Excellent, Jemma, thank you. How was yours?"

"Wonderful," she purred.

I stared at the floor and stiffened in shock when Mason said, "And yours, Naomi?"

He knew my name. Mason Shaw knew my name.

"Naomi?" he prompted.

I swallowed and forced myself to raise my gaze, meeting his hazel eyes with difficulty. "It was good, thank you."

A little shiver ran down my spine. Mason was

giving me a look that I had never seen before from him. Heck, until this moment, I don't think he had ever even looked at me.

Now there was something like appreciation in his gaze as it dropped briefly to my breasts, that were well-hidden beneath my baggy shirt, before rising to my face again.

"Glad to hear it." He grabbed a juice from the fridge and left the kitchen as Jemma eyed his ass with unabashed delight.

When he was gone, she breathed, "Holy shit. Did you see the way he looked at you?"

I flushed. "I don't know what you mean."

Jemma rolled her eyes. "Bullshit, Naomi. You're twenty-three years old – you know when a man wants you."

"Mason Shaw doesn't want me. You – you're being ridiculous."

She frowned at me. "No, I'm not. But be careful, okay? Sleeping with the boss can be dangerous."

"I'm not going to sleep with him!" My voice was too loud, and I cringed before lowering it. "I'm not going to sleep with Mason Shaw."

"Probably a wise move," Jemma said. "I know technically he's not your boss, but you know that he and Dane are super close. Sleeping with Mason would be like sleeping with your boss."

She suddenly fanned her face. "Jesus, what I wouldn't give to be the meat in a Mason/Dane sandwich."

I stared wide-eyed at her. "What do you mean?"

"Oh, please. You can't tell me you haven't heard the rumours."

"They're just rumours," I said.

"Maybe they are and maybe they aren't. But personally, I choose to believe that those two hot studs are exactly what the rumours say they are. I've heard they won't even sleep with a woman unless she agrees to fuck them both. Missy from accounting says she was at a bar last year and she watched the two of them hit on a woman together. She says they had the woman eating out of their hands in less than five minutes and the three of them left together."

She sighed happily. "Could you even imagine what it would be like to be fucked by the both of them?"

When I didn't reply, she elbowed me in the side and grinned. "I can imagine it. In fact, I've imagined it many times."

"I have to go," I mumbled. "Mr. Wilson asked me to come in early to work on the Stanton file."

I hurried out of the kitchen before Jemma could reply. My cheeks were flushed, and my pelvis and breasts were suddenly throbbing.

Get a hold of yourself, I scolded myself fiercely. Even if Mason Shaw had suddenly lost his mind and wanted me, Dane Wilson certainly did not. My boss was sinfully gorgeous with his dark hair and dark eyes, but he was also cold and aloof with me. I was confident he thought I was a complete waste of space. I was lucky he'd even hired me. I had absolutely zero experience and I'd lied horrendously in the interview. I'd spent the first two weeks of my new job, sweating bullets and secretly trying to learn the computer system before my lies were discovered. Even now, three months later, I was terrified that my deception would be discovered even though I had a pretty good handle on my day-to-day tasks.

I needed this job. It paid well and it was my only hope for breaking free of my father's control. Speaking of which, my heart lifted when I saw the plain white envelope sitting on my desk. It was my paycheque.

Payroll was surprised when I requested to be paid by cheque instead of direct deposit, but it was a necessity. My father demanded I hand my earnings over to him, insistent that as a woman I didn't possess the qualities needed to properly manage my money. I couldn't very well refuse, considering I was given permission to get a job based on my promise of working only to help the family and to save for my future wedding.

But I lied about my wage and every payday I used my lunch hour to go to the bank and cash my cheque. I kept back nearly two hundred dollars from each pay, hiding it in a box tucked under a loose floorboard in my room. In another six months or so I'd have enough money for a deposit on an apartment. I would be free of my father, free of the religious cult he had immersed us in, and I'd never have to suffer the humiliation of being nothing more than a man's possession.

I tucked my paycheque into my purse and turned on my computer. Mr. Wilson's office door was closed but I had no doubt he was in there. He always arrived before everyone else and he would be waiting impatiently for the Stanton file. I took a deep breath, pushed away the image of Mason Shaw staring at my breasts, and turned on my computer.

പ്പ ഇ

Naomi

I carried the two mugs of steaming hot tea out of the kitchen and down the hallway. Mr. Wilson had left just before lunch for a client meeting, but he always requested a mug of tea at precisely three-thirty. He wasn't back in the office yet, but I knew he'd be back any minute because his calendar showed a meeting with Mason Shaw at three-thirty.

I stopped in front of Mr. Wilson's closed office door and carefully transferred the second mug of tea to my left hand. I winced a little as the heat of the mugs burned at my fingers. Before I could open the door, it swung open on its own. I had just enough time to get my right arm up and prevent it from smashing me in the face, but the mugs of tea weren't nearly as lucky. The door hit my arm and the mugs, shattering them on contact and spraying hot tea all over my hand, arm and chest. I made a sharp cry of pain before dropping the broken handles.

"Fuck!" Mason Shaw stood in the doorway and he stared at the tea soaking into my white shirt before grabbing my hand and yanking me into Mr. Wilson's office. He moved me swiftly across the room to the private bathroom and pushed me into the small room.

"Son of a bitch," Mason said, and reached for the buttons on my shirt.

"Don't do that!" I slapped at his hands and he frowned at me.

"I need to see if you're burned, Naomi."

He had my shirt unbuttoned and dropped to the floor with surprising quickness. I immediately slapped my arms over my breasts clad in a sensible and boring beige bra. Hot tea had soaked into the fabric, burning my nipples, but I was absolutely mortified to be standing in front of Mason without my shirt. I kept my arms clamped firmly across my breasts.

"Oh, sweetheart, I'm so sorry." He studied my red upper chest.

"I-it's fine, Mr. Shaw," I said. "It was an accident. I need to clean up the mess before it ruins the carpet."

"Stay right where you are, sweetheart."

He dampened the hand towel with cool water and pressed it against my arm and hand. When he pressed it against my upper chest, I couldn't help but flinch. My upper chest and breasts had been splashed with the majority of the hot tea. Mason slipped one arm around me and stroked my bare back soothingly.

"Mr. Shaw, please, I shouldn't be -"

"Shh." He moved the towel in gentle circles against my upper chest. His other hand touched the braid wound around my head. My dark hair was thick and hung nearly to my waist and I was shamefully vain about it. I never wore it down because my father said respectable women always kept their hair neat and tidy in the company of men. Sometimes at night when I was alone in my room, I would release it from its bun or braid and admire the soft silkiness of it.

Mason pulled the towel away and leaned down to examine my chest. His blond hair brushed my chin and I had to press my lips shut against my soft gasp. I'd never been this close to any man before. I breathed in the scent of his cologne as he made a soft noise in the back of his throat.

"My poor sweetheart. Your skin is so delicate," he said.

"It's really okay," I whispered. "I should go and…"

My voice died out in a breathless moan when he pressed his lips against my skin.

"Mr. Shaw, wh-what are you doing?"

"Kissing it better." There was a thin thread of amusement in his voice. My pulse drummed in my veins as he trailed his ridiculously warm lips across my chest.

"Please, you shouldn't do that," I whispered.

"Shouldn't do what? This?" He pressed a kiss against my collarbone, and I moaned when I felt his wet tongue skim across my skin.

"Does that feel better, sweetheart?" He licked my upper chest again.

"I – yes."

"Good." He lifted his head and studied my flushed face. "Do you have any idea how beautiful you are?"

"I'm not beautiful."

"You are," he murmured. "So beautiful."

His gaze dropped to my lips and my mouth turned Sahara Desert dry. He stepped closer, pressing the length of his hard body against mine before brushing his lips against my mouth.

I shivered all over, and he smiled before kissing me again. "So responsive, sweetheart. I knew you would be."

"Mr. Shaw, I -"

"Mason." He licked my upper lip. "Call me Mason."

"M-mason, this is very..."

"Exciting? Arousing? Hot?" He suggested with a small grin.

I was going to say inappropriate but before I could stutter out the word, his mouth was on mine again. For the first time in my life, I had a tongue sliding between my lips.

Holy crap. Mason Shaw was kissing me. French kissing me.

"Kiss me, sweetheart," he breathed against my mouth.

I shouldn't have, I knew that, but the pressure of his mouth was positively intoxicating. I kissed him back hesitantly. I had no idea what I was doing but it must have been okay because Mason groaned again. His arm slid around my waist and he crushed me against his hard body as his kiss turned deeper.

He was sliding his tongue in and out of my mouth, licking and darting and flicking at my tongue with a sweetness that made me moan. I wanted to kiss him forever, wanted to feel the soft brush of his tongue and lips against mine until time just stopped. I had no idea that kissing could feel this good.

"What's going on?"

Dane's deep voice brought me out of my kiss-induced haze. I pushed away from Mason in panic.

"Mr. Wilson, I'm so sorry." I wanted to die of shame. I stared miserably at the floor of the bathroom as he stood in the doorway.

"What's going on, Mason?" Dane repeated.

"I burned her with hot tea," Mason said.

"You did what?" The anger in Dane's voice made me cringe. I took a step back, pressing my ample body against the far wall of the tiny bathroom as Dane crowded into the room.

"Easy, Dane. It was an accident," Mason said. "She was coming into your office, I was coming out, and we collided."

"Does she need to go to the hospital?"

I shook my head. "No, it's not that bad. Mr. Shaw put some, uh, cool water on it and it's already feeling much better."

I was lying. Away from the intoxicating taste of Mason, my upper chest was feeling tender and my breasts, my nipples in particular, were really stinging. I needed to get out of this tiny room filled with two very big men and get to the ladies' room so I could remove my tea-soaked bra and inspect the damage.

I snatched my shirt from the floor but before I could struggle into it, Mason pulled it from my trembling hands. I whirled around to face him with a pleading look.

"You can't wear this, sweetheart. It's soaking

wet."

"It's fine," I said. "Please, can I have my shirt back?"

He shook his head and my eyes widened when I felt Dane's warm breath on the back of my shoulder. "Her bra is soaked as well."

I clamped my arms tightly across my breasts as Mason's gaze dropped to them.

"It isn't," I said.

"It is. Take it off, Naomi," Dane said.

The area between my thighs tingled with shameful anticipation. I couldn't - *shouldn't* – take off my bra even though I suddenly really wanted to do what Dane was telling me. It wasn't proper to be half-naked in front of my boss and his best friend. I stared anxiously at Mason as I said, "No, I – I can't."

"You can." Dane's hard body was touching mine now and I gasped when I felt his fingers brush across the clasp of my bra. "We need to see your breasts, Naomi."

Even as he was speaking, his nimble fingers were unhooking my bra. I made another nervous squeak when he slid his fingers under the straps at my shoulders.

"Lower your arms."

He spoke quietly but the dark command in his voice had me dropping my arms immediately. He slipped the bra from my body and I closed my eyes in a combination of shame and desire as I stood half-naked in front of two men.

"So fucking gorgeous," Mason crooned.

My eyes popped open. He was staring at my

breasts with a look of pure hunger and my body reacted instantly. My nipples peaked, and there was a surge of wetness between my thighs as my pussy instinctively smoothed a path for Mason.

Dane's big hands cupped my breasts. I moaned and sagged back against him as fire licked at my nerve endings. He lifted my breasts, testing their weight before squeezing them lightly.

"Are your nipples sore?" he murmured into my ear before licking the curve of it.

I moaned again, my hands clutching helplessly at Dane's forearms as he licked my neck.

"Are they, baby?" he said.

Incapable of speech, I nodded. He soothed his thumbs over my nipples before glancing at Mason.

"Mason, help her."

"My pleasure." Mason dropped my shirt to the floor. His blond head dipped lower and I pressed back against Dane's body, barely registering the hardness I felt against my ass.

"I don't think -"

"Shh, baby." Dane was still cupping my breasts and Holy Mother of Mary did it feel good. "We just want to help."

He lifted my breasts even higher, guiding my nipple to Mason's mouth. I cried out when Mason sucked tenderly at my nipple. His mouth was hot and wet, and the stinging was instantly soothed by the laving of his tongue.

"Fuck, Dane," Mason muttered against my breast. "Her nipples are incredible."

He sucked and nibbled and licked as I pressed my ass against Dane and made soft cries of need.

Oh God, had I ever felt anything this good before?

"Look at me, Naomi." Dane's voice demanded obedience and I tilted my head up. Immediately his mouth descended on mine, his tongue pressing against my lips. I moaned helplessly and parted my lips as he slanted his mouth over mine and thrust his tongue in deep.

His kisses were nothing like Mason's. There was no softness to his touch, just hardness and desperate need, and I submitted immediately to his dominance. There was something right about allowing him to have control and take what he wanted from me. I returned his kiss eagerly as he slid his hand over the curve of my belly to the elastic waist of my skirt.

Mason continued to lick and nibble at my breasts, his hot mouth bringing goosebumps to my flesh, as Dane pushed his hand past my skirt and into my cotton panties. His hand cupped my hot core and his fingers glided through the shameful amount of liquid that had gathered there. He groaned into my mouth.

"She's so fucking wet, Mason."

"Good," Mason said against my breast.

"Are you wet for us, baby?" Dane said. "Does your pussy want our cocks?"

I tried to close my legs as he stroked the wet lips of my warmth.

"No," he growled. "Keep your legs open for me, Naomi."

"Mr. Wilson," I whispered. "This isn't right. I shouldn't be -"

He kissed me again as the tips of his fingers

brushed the tiny, throbbing bundle of nerves between my legs. My reaction was hot and immediate. My back arched and I cried out into his mouth as he rubbed it again.

"She's so damn responsive," Dane rumbled.

"I know." Mason grinned up at him. "It's the fucking hottest thing I've ever seen."

"Please," I whispered.

"Please what, baby?" Dane sucked on my bottom lip.

"I want more," I moaned shamelessly.

"More of this?" His fingers touched my clit again and I jerked against him as Mason chose that moment to bite my nipple.

"Oh! Oh yes," I said frantically.

"Whatever you want," he growled before rubbing and tugging on my clit. I shook and writhed against him as a strange tension built in my belly.

"Please, oh please!" I cried out.

I couldn't think, couldn't breathe. Mason had pushed my breasts together and his hot mouth was slipping back and forth, sucking each nipple into an aching hardness, as Dane continued to circle and rub my clit.

The delicious tension was building, and I stared at Dane in a panic. "What – what's happening to me?"

His eyes widened and his fingers slowed to a stop as he glanced at Mason. "Mason, I don't think she -"

"Fuck, Dane. Shut your mouth and make her cum. I need to see it," Mason said.

"Dane? Please help me. I can't – the ache – I can't stand the ache," I whispered.

He cursed before covering my mouth with his. I was so close but to what I didn't know. I only knew that if he didn't touch me, if he didn't help me, I would go completely mad.

His fingers pinched that hard button between my legs, pinched it and then rubbed it and suddenly I was falling. I screamed, the sound muffled by his mouth as the most incredible rush of pleasure swept through me. It made my limbs shake with the intensity and I would have fallen to the floor if Dane's strong arm hadn't been hooked around my waist. My eyes were squeezed shut, my mouth filled with Dane's tongue, and my breasts held firmly by Mason's large hands as his fingers caressed my rock-hard nipples.

"Holy shit," Mason said when I finally stopped shuddering and writhing between them and sagged against Dane. Mason still cupped my breasts and I was only vaguely aware of Dane's middle finger sliding down and breaching my tight entrance.

"Did you see that, Dane?" Mason said. "That was hands-down the best fucking orgasm I've ever watched a woman have. I need to fuck her right now."

"Mason." Dane's finger probed inside of me and I winced and tried to close my legs as he withdrew his finger. "Jesus, Mason, I think she's a -"

"Mr. Wilson?" Our receptionist's voice coming from the phone intercom on Dane's desk was tinny and low but the three of us froze like she was in the room with us.

"Mr. Wilson?"

Dane stepped away from me and strode into the office.

"What is it?" he barked.

"Your four o'clock is here. Should I send him to your office?"

"No," he said. "Put him in the boardroom."

"Yes, sir."

The intercom clicked off, and I backed away as Mason reached for me. I bent and snatched my wet shirt and bra from the floor, holding them against my chest as Mason frowned at me.

"Sweetheart? What's wrong?"

"Please leave," I whispered. The pleasure I had felt at their touch had disappeared, and I was left with a sick feeling in the pit of my stomach. What had I done? I had allowed my boss and his best friend to – to touch me, to make me…

My mind skittered away from the word and shame swept through me. What if my father found out? What if he told the church members? I had seen that once when I was only thirteen. A young woman, barely nineteen, was brought in front of the entire congregation and forced to confess her sins of fornication. She had wept and shook through the entire confession, and I'd stared grimly at my knees, unable to watch her shame as the other church members stared at her in stony silence.

I couldn't do that. I couldn't stand in front of my parents and the entire church and admit to what I let, no what I *wanted*, Mason and Dane to do to me. I'd already decided that once I was free of my father and free of the church and its rules, I would find a nice boy and have sex with him. It was one more way to rebel against my father and his constant reminder that nice girls waited until marriage, that nice girls didn't date – they courted. Kissing, touching, having sex was meant for the marriage bed only.

But there was something entirely different about meeting a nice boy and sleeping with him compared to letting two men feel me up in the office bathroom. I clamped my mouth shut against the whimper that wanted to escape.

"Please leave," I repeated.

"Mason, leave her," Dane said.

Mason frowned at him. "Dane, I can't leave her like this. She's upset and -"

"Leave her, I said," Dane snarled. He all but yanked Mason out of the bathroom and shut the door. I dressed quickly, grimacing at the cold material, before easing the door open.

Dane and Mason were standing silently in the middle of the office and I stared at the floor as I walked past them. My cheeks were burning, and I was very close to vomiting.

"Go home, Naomi," Dane said gruffly.

I froze, my heart stopping in my chest for a moment before galloping back into action. I whipped around and stared pleadingly at Dane.

"I'm so sorry. Please, I'm so sorry. Please don't fire me. I won't say a word about what happened and I – I'll never go near you again. Just please don't fire me. I really need this job. Please, Mr. Wilson. Please."

The words tumbled out of my mouth as the hot tears leaked down my cheeks. I could only imagine how utterly pathetic I looked with my red face, my shirt clinging wetly to my large breasts and belly, and the tears spilling from my eyes. I didn't care. I would get down on my knees and beg for my job if that's what it took. Without this job, I was doomed.

"You're not fired," Dane said quickly, holding Mason back when he started forward. "I just meant go home for the day."

I stared hesitantly at him and he said, "Go home, Naomi, but I expect you to be back in the office at seven-thirty tomorrow. I'll need you to work on the Stanton file again."

My entire body trembling with relief, I turned and fled.

കം ൶

Mason

"What the fuck, Dane?" I turned on my best friend the moment the office door shut behind Naomi. "I know you're a fucking cruel bastard, but you went too far, you asshole. She needed to be held, to be soothed and shown -"

"No," Dane said, "she needed to get away from us. You saw the look on her face, Mason. She was both incredibly ashamed and terrified by what happened."

I stared uncertainly at Dane. Truthfully, I was so wrapped up in Naomi's soft body, in the feel of her nipples in my mouth, and the sound of her cries, I hadn't really noticed the look on her face. All I'd wanted was to sink my dick deep into her warm pussy and watch as she climaxed around my cock.

"Are you sure?" I said.

Dane nodded before grimacing and adjusting his cock through his suit pants. "I think that was her first orgasm."

"Bullshit," I said. "There's no fucking way it was her first. How old is she again? Twenty-five?"

"Twenty-three."

"There's no way," I repeated. "Even if she'd never had one with a guy, you know damn well she would have masturbated by this age."

"She didn't know what was happening," Dane said. "When I was touching her, she looked right at me and asked what was happening to her."

I stared silently at Dane as he rubbed his fingers against his temple in a gesture I recognized well. "She's a virgin, Mason. I'm sure of it."

"Well, shit."

"Yeah," Dane said. "We can't go any further with this."

"Damn right, we can't," I said. "Listen, I know we were both excited by her innocence but there's a difference between being shy and innocent and being a goddamn virgin."

"I know."

"We aren't the type to deflower the blushing virgin so don't even start getting any ideas."

"I know," Dane repeated.

"Not that it wouldn't be fucking amazing to show her how to please a man. She's naturally submissive, did you notice?"

"Yes."

"Really submissive. Could you imagine how she'd look restrained to the bed? Clamps on those gorgeous nipples of hers and a collar around her throat?"

"Mason," Dane's voice was strangled, and he pulled at the front of his pants, "we have a meeting. Stop talking about this."

"You're right. We have to stay away from her. Keep it strictly professional from now on."

"Yeah," Dane grunted.

I glanced at him. "Can you?"

He nodded and then scowled at me when I arched my eyebrows in disbelief. "I can, Mason. Now, c'mon, let's get this fucking meeting over with so I can go home and have a cold shower."

Chapter Three

Naomi

"Naomi? Come into the family room, please." My mother's voice called down the hallway.

I groaned inwardly and slipped out of my shoes. "Give me a minute."

"No," my father barked. "Get in here."

Leaving my jacket on to cover my tea-stained shirt, I entered the family room. My father was sitting in his chair and my mother was hovering next to the couch.

"You're home early," she said.

"Um, it wasn't busy at work," I said. "My boss said I could leave early."

"Sit down, Naomi," my father said.

I sat on the couch. My mother's face was pale and uneasy.

"What's wrong?" I said.

"Nothing's wrong," my father said.

I stared silently at him until he looked away. "You're quitting your job tomorrow."

"What? No, I – I can't."

His gaze returned to mine, his nostrils flaring and anger flickering in his eyes at my disobedience. "You can and you will."

"But... but the money," I said. "I know money is tight right now and I know my paycheque helps. Here." I dug the money from my wallet and held it out.

My mother drifted forward and took the wad of cash, handing it to my father who made it disappear into his pocket.

"You're quitting your job tomorrow, Naomi, and there will be no further discussion on it."

"No," I said. "I won't."

My father's eyes widened, and he turned to my mother. "See, Alice? I told you this would happen."

"Josiah, you have to tell her. She's going to find out," my mother said.

"Find out what?" There was a very bad feeling rising in my stomach. "What's going on?"

My father nodded to my mother and she said, "Naomi, your father – I mean, *we* – are having a bigger financial problem then you think."

"So, then I should keep working," I said. "The money is -"

"It's not enough," my mother said. "Satan has been hard at work in this household. Your father is a good man but, like all men, not completely immune to temptation."

"What are you talking about?" I said.

"You father owes a debt to Deacon Dennison," my mother replied.

"The head deacon of the church?" I frowned at her in confusion. "How?"

"Your father was tempted into gambling and he, unfortunately, spent a great deal of money. Deacon Dennison loaned us the money we needed to pay our bills and now he's requesting his loan be paid in full. Fortunately for us, he's willing to accept a different form of payment."

"I don't understand," I said.

My mother licked her lips. "Deacon Dennison is looking for a wife."

"So?" I said. "What does that have to do with us?"

My mother didn't answer. My entire body went cold as sudden understanding flooded through me.

"No," I whispered through lips that had gone numb. "You wouldn't."

"Deacon Dennison is a well-respected man in the church and will treat you well," my mother said.

"He's Dad's age and – and fat and ugly!" I shouted.

My mother flinched, and my father jumped up from his chair. "Do not speak of your elders in such a manner, Naomi!"

"Are you kidding me?" I was still shouting. "You're selling me off to some perverted old man in order to pay your gambling debts and you expect me to be respectful?"

He strode across the room and I cried out when he slapped me across the face. My head flew back, and I cupped my stinging cheek as he glared at me. "Keep your mouth shut, Naomi!"

"Josiah, please," my mother said, her voice high

with anxiety, "you must be calm."

My father grabbed me by the shoulders. "You will marry Deacon Dennison, Naomi. Do you hear me? If you don't, we'll lose our home. We'll lose everything and it will be your fault."

"How is it my fault that you gambled away -"

He shook me again, making me wince. "I will not have my child speak to me this way! You will do as I tell you! Or are you so selfish you wish to see your mother living on the streets, begging for food and money, perhaps selling her body to any man who will take her?"

My cheek throbbed and burned as my mother paced behind us.

"Do you?" my father roared.

"No."

He released me and smoothed his hair down. "This will be a good match, Naomi. You'll see."

"How much?" I asked dully.

"What?"

"How much did you sell your own daughter for?"

My father's face reddened, and he clenched his hands into tight fists. "That's none of your business."

"Tell me."

"Twenty-five grand."

My mouth dropped open and I stared wordlessly at him. I flinched when he reached out, but he only stroked the top of my head. "Tomorrow morning your mother will drive you to work and you will quit your job. Deacon Dennison will be dropping by in the afternoon to meet with you. You will be respectful and obedient and make a good impression. Do you understand?"

I nodded again, huddling against the couch as my father held out his hand. "Give me your purse."

"What?"

"Give me your purse."

I handed it over and he gave it to my mother. "Lock this in our room."

My plan to wait until they fell asleep then jump in my car and drive away, faded as my mother carried my purse out of the room.

"You're making a sacrifice for your family, Naomi," my father said. "Our Lord will be very pleased, and you will find your reward in the Kingdom of Heaven."

I didn't reply and my father's face twisted into something ugly and cruel. "You are dismissed."

I jumped up and ran to my room as loud sobs broke from my throat.

༺ ༻

Dane

I ignored the soft knock on my office door. It was almost seven thirty and I was standing anxiously at the window, scanning the employee parking lot for Naomi's familiar form. She hadn't arrived yet and my stomach was churning with nerves. What if she never returned? What if Mason and I had frightened her so badly that she simply walked away.

She won't. She begged for her job yesterday, remember? She won't just quit.

There was another soft knock and I shouted irritably for them to come in.

"Mr. Wilson?"

Naomi's low voice made my cock harden. I whipped around, relief flooding through me. "Good morning, Naomi."

She stood in front of my desk, keeping her eyes on the floor. "Mr. Wilson, I'm sorry, I have to -"

"What happened to your face?" I started around the desk, stopping when she backed away.

"Nothing," she said.

"Bullshit. It's bruised. What happened, Naomi?"

She ignored my question. "I'm sorry but I'm here to give you my resignation."

Panic flowed through me. "No."

She blinked at me, her lovely blue eyes were already filling with tears, and stammered, "W-what?"

"No, I'm not accepting your resignation."

"You... you have to," she whispered.

"No, I fucking don't." I picked up my phone and dialed Mason's extension.

"Mason, I need you. Now," I barked when he answered. I hung up without waiting for his reply.

"Mr. Wilson, please, you need to take this." She was holding out a piece of paper, her hand shaking visibly.

"Yesterday you were begging for your job and today you're quitting. Tell me why."

"I – I can't," she said.

"Yes, you can." I started toward her, my gut clenching when she skittered away from me.

"I really can't." Now the tears were dripping down her face, and I breathed a sigh of relief when Mason skidded into the room.

"Dane? What's wrong?"

He stared in surprise at Naomi before closing the door and walking toward her. "Sweetheart? What happened to your cheek?"

"She's quitting," I announced. My hands white knuckled the back of my office chair, and I gritted my teeth as Mason made a soft soothing noise.

"Oh, sweetheart, no. Don't quit. What happened yesterday was our fault, not yours. We won't let it happen again, okay?"

He eased his arm around her shoulders – she wasn't afraid of him I thought morosely – and led her to the couch.

"I'm not quitting because of what happened yesterday," she said.

Mason glanced at me as he sat Naomi down on the couch. I started toward them and he shook his head minutely. He was right. If I tried to sit down it would just make her more nervous, but fuck was it a punch to the gut knowing that I frightened her.

"Then why are you quitting?" he said in a gentle tone I'd never be able to mimic.

"I can't tell you," she said.

"Of course, you can. Naomi," he placed his finger under her chin and tilted her face to his, "tell us why you're quitting."

Her bottom lip trembled. "My father is making me quit."

"You're twenty-three years old," I said. "You're a little old to be letting your father tell you what to do."

She flinched, and Mason glared at me. I took another step back. I shouldn't have admonished her, but I was feeling uncharacteristically panicky and uncertain, and I had no idea how to process it.

"You don't understand." Her voice was flat and dull. "Men like you couldn't possibly understand."

"Then help us understand," Mason said. "Tell us everything."

"My mother is waiting downstairs for me," she said. "I don't have time."

"Yes, you do, sweetheart," Mason coaxed. "Tell us."

She hesitated and then said, "My father is very religious. We belong to a church that is actually a cult."

I swore under my breath and Mason glared at me when Naomi flinched. "Go on, sweetheart."

"When I was twenty, my older sister, Joy, started disobeying. She snuck out at night, she met up with – with boys, and she started drinking and having sex. My father sent her away. He married her off to a man who specialized in disciplining women who had strayed from the path of God. Joy was his fifth wife."

"Fuck," I snarled as Mason rubbed Naomi's arm.

She stared at her hands. "I'm a good girl but I knew it was only a matter of time before my father married me off as well. There's a boy at our church, Jeremiah, and he was interested in courting me, but I didn't like him. He reminded me too much of my father."

She rubbed her hands together like they were cold. "It's very important that we marry and have babies and at twenty-three, I'm already much older than most of the single girls in our church. I figured that my father would force me to court Jeremiah, but he hasn't pushed me too much on it. I thought it was because I was working, you know? I convinced my parents to let me get a job and they agreed to it because they needed money. I didn't know at the time, but my father has a – a gambling problem."

Mason pulled her a little closer as she said, "I lied in the interview. I said I knew the computer system, but I really didn't. It was the only way I could think to get the job. I'm sorry for lying."

She peeked at me and I said, "It's fine, baby."

"My parents make me give them my paycheque, but I keep some of it. Every pay I hide a couple hundred dollars in my room. In another few months, I would have had enough for a rent deposit on an apartment. I would be free."

Her voice broke and Mason kissed her forehead as she started to sob. "Only last night my father informed me that I have to pay back a debt he owes to the head deacon of our church. He's fifty and balding and ugly and gross."

She suddenly clutched at Mason's hand. "I said no that I wouldn't help him. But he owes Deacon Dennison twenty-five thousand dollars. If my father has to pay that back, he said that we'll lose the house and my mother will be forced into prostitution."

"Jesus Christ," Mason muttered before staring at

me.

I stared at him with a sick look of anger as Naomi wiped at the tears on her cheeks. "Luckily for us, Deacon Dennison is willing to accept an alternate payment."

"What do you mean?" Mason asked.

"You," I said, anger flickering through my veins. "Your father is selling you to this asshole to pay off his debt, isn't he?"

"Yes. He's coming by this afternoon to discuss the," she laughed bitterly, "marriage arrangement."

"No fucking way," Mason said. "That is not fucking happening."

He stood and paced back and forth. "A man can't just sell his daughter like that, Dane. We need to call the police."

"No!" Naomi jumped to her feet. "Don't you dare call the police. If you do that, my mother, she'll…"

She stared pleadingly at us. "She's still my mother."

"You can't do this, Naomi," Mason said. "Sweetheart, I don't know what your crazy religion has told you, but fathers can't just sell their daughters like cattle."

She backed toward the door. "I have no choice. I have no money and no place to live. I shouldn't have told you. I'm sorry, I need to go. Thank you for giving me a job and for, uh, yesterday. I, "her cheeks flushed bright red, "I liked it very much. Goodbye, Mason. Goodbye, Mr. Wilson."

"Naomi, wait!"

Mason lunged forward but she had already

skittered out of the office and closed the door.

"Mason, stop," I said when he opened the door.

"Are you fucking crazy, Dane? We can't let this happen."

"I know but going to the police isn't going to help. You saw the look on her face when we mentioned the police. She'll hate us if we call them."

"I don't fucking care!" Mason slammed the door shut. "Let her hate us! We can't just sit by and let this happen."

"We're not going to," I said grimly. "I have a better idea."

"What's that?"

"We're going to buy Naomi for ourselves."

❧ ❧

Mason

"Be cool," I muttered to Dane as we climbed the steps to the small bungalow.

"Yeah," he said. "Ring the goddamn bell."

I rang the doorbell and we waited impatiently. Footsteps approached and the door opened. Naomi's mouth dropped open and I smiled at her.

"Hello, Naomi."

"Wh- what are you doing here?"

"Can we come in?"

She shook her head. "No, I'm sorry."

Dane grunted in anger and pushed past me. He wrapped his arms around Naomi's waist and lifted her out of the way.

"Mr. Wilson, stop!" she whisper-shouted as he

set her down and strode down the hallway. She chased after him and I followed them both.

Dane ground to a halt as we heard a voice drift from the first doorway. "She's a good girl. Pure and untouched and eager to obey. You won't have any problems with her."

"So, she's a virgin then?" A nasally and high-pitched voice replied.

"Yes, of course."

"Good."

Naomi turned bright red and Dane's back stiffened.

"Easy, Dane," I murmured as he stepped into the doorway.

"Who are you?" Two men, one short and bald with a large belly and the other tall and skinny stared at us.

"Mr. Morris?" I brushed past Dane and held my hand out.

The taller man automatically shook my hand. I tamped down my urge to squeeze until his fingers snapped. "I'm Mason Shaw, and this is my associate Dane Wilson. Your daughter works for us."

"No, she doesn't," he said. "She quit."

"Yes, she did quit this morning," I said as a woman with eyes the same colour as Naomi's and long, graying hair entered the room with a tray of cookies.

"Josiah?" She stared uncertainly at us. "What's going on?"

"These are Naomi's bosses." Josiah glanced at the other man. "Deacon Dennison, forgive the intrusion. I'll have these men leave and we can continue -"

"Yes," I said. "Please continue on with the sale of your daughter, Mr. Morris."

Naomi and her mother made identical gasps of dismay as her father's face turned red. "Who do you think you are?"

"I've told you who we are," I said.

"Get out of my home. Right now, before I call the police."

Dane snarled at him. "You're lucky we don't fucking call the police, you goddamn asshole."

"Mr. Morris, I understand you owe," I pointed to the pervert beside him, "this sick bastard a debt of twenty-five grand, is that right?"

"What did you tell them, Naomi?" her father snarled.

She cringed back when he started toward her. "What did you say?"

Dane stepped in front of Naomi, blocking her from her father's angry gaze. "Take another step toward her and I'll break both your arms."

Her father's face paled. "Alice, call the police."

"You might want to wait a minute, Alice," I said as Naomi's mother set the tray on the coffee table. "I think your husband will want to hear what we have to offer."

"What are you talking about?" Naomi's father said.

I held up the small leather bag I was carrying in my left hand. "This bag contains a hundred grand in cash. That's more than enough to pay that perverted prick his twenty-five thousand and give you and your wife a little nest egg."

"You – you're just going to give me a hundred thousand dollars?" Naomi's father's face lit up with greed. It was all I could do not to drop the bag and punch his face into a bloody mess.

"Not quite," I replied. "We'll give you the hundred grand, if you give us Naomi."

Her mother gasped in horror. "No, no, we won't do that."

"Be quiet, Alice," her father said. He glanced at Deacon Dennison who frowned.

"Josiah, we had an agreement."

Her father hesitated, and I opened the bag and showed him the bundles of cash. "A hundred grand, Mr. Morris. All yours and all you have to do is give us Naomi."

"Deal," he said suddenly. Fuck, the urge to kick his ass was nearly overpowering.

"Josiah, no!" her mother said. "We don't even know these men!"

Dane snorted dark laughter. "I guarantee you she'll have a much better life with us than with that fucking pervert. Naomi, get your things."

Her face bloodless, Naomi stood motionless behind him. Dane touched her shoulder. "Get your things, Naomi. You're leaving with us."

She stumbled out of the room as her mother clutched at her husband's arm. "Josiah, please, you can't do this."

"It's done, Alice. Be quiet!" he said.

Naomi returned after only a few minutes. She held nothing in her hand but her purse and an envelope.

"Where are your things?" Dane said.

"There isn't anything I want to take with me," she said.

Dane studied the paleness of her face and the faint bruise that graced her cheek. Before I could stop him, he moved forward and grabbed her father by his shirt collar. He dragged him up until their noses were nearly touching.

"Naomi belongs to us now. If you go anywhere near her, if you ever touch her again, I'll kill you. Do you understand?"

Her father stared terrified at him and Dane shook him roughly. "Do you understand, you fucking pig?"

"Yes!" He stumbled back when Dane released him. Dane turned and took Naomi by the arm, leading her toward the doorway.

"Naomi?" her mother said.

Naomi stared silently at her for a moment. "Goodbye, Mom."

I dropped the bag of money on the floor and followed Dane and Naomi down the hallway, out the front door, and into the late afternoon light.

Chapter Four

Naomi

"Where are we?" I asked as Dane pulled up in front of a large iron gate. He pushed a button on a remote clipped to the visor and the gate swung open. We drove down a winding driveway as the gate closed behind us.

"Our home," Mason said.

"You live together?"

"We do," Mason said.

Dane stopped in front of a large colonial style home. I studied the massive pillars and the front porch as Dane shut off the car. Mason hopped out of the back seat and opened my door. I unbuckled my seat belt and climbed out, not resisting when Mason took my hand and led me up the steps and across the wide porch. He opened the door and I followed him inside to the foyer. I barely had time to study my surroundings before Mason was leading me to the kitchen.

"Wow," I said as Mason urged me to sit at the

island. "Your place is really nice."

The kitchen was gorgeous with modern white cupboards, grey quartz countertops, and stainless-steel appliances. Teal accents were scattered throughout the room.

"Thank you." Mason glanced at Dane.

Dane grabbed a bottle of water from the fridge and opened it before handing it to me. "Drink this, baby."

"Thank you." I sipped at the water before setting it on the island. "Are you guys millionaires?"

"No," Mason said.

"We do all right for ourselves," Dane said.

"All right?" I laughed or tried to laugh – it came out with a weirdly hysterical and jagged note to it. "You just bought me for a hundred grand, and you do *all right* for yourselves?"

Mason winced before sitting next to me. "Naomi -"

"You shouldn't have done that," I said. "I don't have a hundred grand to pay you back."

"We don't want your money," Dane said.

"Then what do you want?" I asked.

Dane looked at Mason and I made another one of those jagged little laughs. "Never mind, I can guess. I know you heard my father tell Deacon Dennison I was a virgin. Does that increase or decrease my value to you?"

"Stop," Dane said. "We don't -"

"I'm guessing increase." I slid off the stool. Mason reached for me and I pulled away. I clutched at the side of the island while my heart pounded in my chest. I had no idea what was happening to me. I was terrified and furious and heartbroken all at the same time, and my entire body shook as I stared at the two men. "So, I guess the only question is – which one of you ponied up the hundred grand? I assume he's the lucky one who gets to screw me first?"

"Sweetheart, that isn't what we're looking for," Mason said.

"Bullcrap!" I spat at him. "You paid money for me because you – you want to screw me and when you found out my father was selling me like cattle, you figured this was the easiest way. Well, I hate to be the one to share bad news, but you're going to be awfully disappointed. I'm not just a virgin – I'm a virgin with zero experience. Do you understand? I don't know how to kiss, I don't know how to touch a guy. I've never even masturbated!"

I was shouting now, and tears were flowing fast and furious down my cheeks. It hurt to breathe, and inner me was recoiling in horror at the things I was saying to the men in front of me, but I couldn't seem to stop.

"I'm not worth a hundred grand!" I shouted. "I'm not even worth a hundred dollars and -"

"Naomi, enough."

Dane's low voice broke through my confusion and anger and fear. I ground to a halt.

"That's enough," he repeated, and I burst into tears and sunk to my knees on the floor.

Mason was immediately next to me. He sat down and pulled me into his lap as Dane crouched next to us. I buried my face in Mason's chest and wept.

"He-he-he sold me! My own father sold me like I was nothing, to men he didn't even know!" I sobbed. "What's wrong with me?"

"Nothing," Mason said. "There's nothing wrong with you. Your father is a monster."

I sobbed even harder and Mason rubbed my back before rocking me back and forth like I was a small child. "It's okay, sweetheart. It's okay."

Despite my shame and embarrassment, I cried for nearly fifteen minutes. Mason's shirt was wet, and my face was a hot, red mess when I finally stopped crying. A tissue was shoved into my hand and I wiped my face and blew my nose before trying to slide from Mason's lap. His hand tightened on my hip and he held me still before kissing my forehead.

"Sweetheart, I know you're tired and upset and want to rest, but you need to hear this first. Okay?"

I nodded and stared at my hands as Mason kissed my forehead again. "We didn't buy you from your father for sex. We paid him the money because we believed it was the only way to help you. We are not expecting you to have sex with us. Is that clear?"

I nodded again as a weird trickle of disappointment went through me. What was wrong with me? Did I actually want them to force me to have sex with them until my debt was paid off? Why did the idea of being Mason and Dane's personal whore suddenly sound so appealing?

"We mean it, Naomi," Dane said.

"I know," I said. "Listen, I should go."

"Go where?" Dane asked.

"I don't know but I'll figure it out. I know I handed in my resignation letter this morning, but my father forced me to do it. I didn't want to resign."

"You still have your job," Dane said.

I breathed a sigh of relief. "Thank you so much. I realize that I owe you a lot of money, but do you think we could work out a payment plan? I can give you a portion of my paycheque every two weeks until it's paid off."

I almost laughed out loud at how stupid I sounded but I had no idea what else to tell them. I owed them an astronomical amount of money and I would need the rest of my life to pay it off.

"You're not paying us back the money," Mason said.

"What... no, I have to."

"You don't."

"I do," I insisted. "A hundred grand is a lot of money and -"

"You're not paying us back and that's final." Dane's voice was perfectly calm, but I could hear the anger in it. I flinched like he had shouted at me. A look of dismay immediately crossed his face and he stood and backed away. Guilt flooded through me but before I could apologize, Mason cupped my face and made me look at him.

"Dane and I don't want your money, sweetheart."

"What do you want?" I whispered.

"For you to be happy and safe," he said. "We want you to stay with us."

"You want me to live with you?"

"Yes. We have plenty of space. You'll have your own bedroom and bathroom. Hell, this place is big enough that you never even need to see either of us if you don't want to. We know you don't have enough money for an apartment. Live with us, save up some money, and you can go from there. Okay?"

"Why are you doing this?" I said. "Why are you being so nice to me? You don't even know me."

Mason brushed his hand over my braid. "You're a good person, sweetheart. You deserve to have someone be nice to you."

"I can't live with two men," I said.

"Why not?" Dane said.

"Well, because it isn't proper. My father won't allow me to -"

"Your father can't tell you what to do," Dane said irritably. "You're a grown woman and can make your own decisions."

I flinched again, and Dane sighed and rubbed at his forehead. Mason eased me off his lap before standing and pulling me to my feet. "We really do just want to help, Naomi. We promise you do not have to have sex with us."

I stared silently at him before saying, "What if I want to have sex with you?"

There was a sharp inhale behind me. I turned to see that Dane had inched closer until he was standing directly behind me. I turned bright red. What on earth possessed me to say that? What happened at the office was amazing, but despite what I yelled hysterically at them earlier, I knew they didn't want me anymore. Why would they? They had a lot of experience and being with a woman who didn't know the first thing about sex or intimacy wouldn't interest them. Besides, nice girls didn't want their first time to be with two men.

I shivered all over when Dane reached out and rubbed his thumb along the line of my jaw. His dark eyes studied my mouth and I immediately parted my lips. He groaned under his breath and Mason said, "Dane, wait."

Dane ignored him completely. His arm snaked around my waist and he pulled me up against his big body. I stared mutely at him as he rubbed my jawline again.

"You want to be fucked by us, baby?" he rumbled as his other hand cupped my ass and squeezed. "You want my dick in your pussy and Mason's dick in your ass?"

"Dane!" Mason's voice held a warning note. Dane made an actual growl when Mason pulled me away from him.

"I'm sorry," I said. "I shouldn't have said that. I didn't mean to, um, be a," I struggled for the word, "tease."

"You weren't," Mason said. "Don't worry, it's fine."

It didn't look fine with Dane. In fact, he looked royally pissed off. I pressed against Mason when Dane crossed his arms over his chest and glared at both of us.

"Sweetheart, I'm going to take you to your room now, okay? Unless you're hungry? We can make you something to eat before -"

"No," I said, "I'm not hungry. I just – I feel like I need to be by myself for a while. If that's okay?" I was suddenly overwhelmed and tired and if I spent one more moment with either Mason or Dane, I would either start bawling again or worse - beg them to have sex with me.

"Of course." Mason took my hand. "Come with me and I'll show you to your room."

With one last anxious glance at Dane, I followed Mason out of the kitchen.

ờ ·6

Dane

"You need to chill out around her, Dane."

Mason poured himself a cup of coffee before sitting next to me at the table. It was early the next morning. Naomi had spent the entire evening in her bedroom and wouldn't eat dinner. I had spent the entire evening drinking whiskey and contemplating how to get away with murdering her father.

"I'm angry," I said.

"Yeah, I am too. I'd like to beat the shit out of her father for what he's done to her," Mason said. "But Naomi thinks you're angry with her."

Frustration rolled off of me in waves. Mason said, "You know we can't have sex with her. She's submissive because her father beat or bullied it into her. She needs therapy, not two Doms in bed."

"I want her." Even to myself I sounded like a petulant child. Before Mason could say anything, I said, "Yeah, I know what I sound like. But I think we should at least talk to her first. We can tell her that we're Doms, explain what it is to her and she can make her choice. She's sheltered and naïve, but she's smart and capable of making her own decisions."

"I don't think it's a good idea."

"I don't care!" I said. "I need her, Mason. I don't know why, and I don't fucking understand it, but I need her. I can't eat, I can't sleep, I can't fucking *think* about anything but her. We have to at least talk to her."

"What if she says no?"

"Then I'll tell her we won't be dominate. We'll just have vanilla sex with her."

"We?" Mason cocked his eyebrow at me. "Can you even do vanilla sex anymore?"

"Yes," I snapped."

"What if she still says no?"

"She won't." My confidence was only half faked.

Mason stared thoughtfully at me and I took my own sip of coffee. "When she says yes to fucking us -"

"If," Mason said.

"Fine. If she says yes to fucking us, I want to be her first," I said. "It's important to me."

"Why?"

"I don't know," I said honestly. "It just is. It's special and…"

Fuck, I sounded like a goddamn pussy.

Mason thought about it for a moment before nodding. "Yeah, okay. If she even agrees to have sex with us."

"She will," I said.

"She may not want you to be her first. You know that, right?"

I stared into my coffee. "Yeah, I know."

"Just try and be a little gentler around her," Mason advised. "She's attracted to you, that's obvious, but you're too intense for her."

"I'll try," I said. "If she'll ever come out of her bedroom and -"

"Good morning."

Naomi's soft voice made my cock stiffen immediately. She stepped tentatively into the kitchen, and Mason jumped up and pulled out the chair next to him. Afraid she'd see the obvious tent in the front of my pants, I stayed where I was.

"Thank you," she said.

She sat down and Mason said, "Do you want coffee?"

"Oh no, I can't," she said. "My father says that coffee is for weak-willed people and..." She cleared her throat. "Yes, please. I would love some coffee."

Mason poured her a cup of coffee and brought it to the table along with milk and sugar. He set it in front of her and she gripped the handle of the mug with obvious apprehension.

"Sweetheart, you don't have to drink the coffee if you don't want to," Mason said.

"I want to," she said. "I want to – to start trying and doing new things."

Her gaze landed on me and when I spoke, my voice was low and filled with obvious need, "You can try or do whatever you want, baby."

"Dane!" Mason said.

I could hear the exasperation in my best friend's voice, and I tried to reign in my lust. I seemed to lose all control when I was around Naomi.

"Sorry," I muttered.

"It's fine," Naomi said. She took a sip of coffee and both Mason and I grinned at the look on her face.

"It's so bitter," she said.

"Try putting in some sugar and milk," Mason said.

She added both and sipped at it again before adding another two teaspoons of sugar. She stirred, sipped, and then smiled at us. "That's better."

"You like it sweet," Mason said with a laugh.

"How did you sleep?" I asked.

"Not great," she admitted.

"Why don't you try and get some more rest after breakfast," Mason said.

"What? No, I have to go to work," Naomi said. "I already missed yesterday and it's busy this week and -"

"You can have the rest of the week off," I said.

"No, I can't do that."

"Yes, you can," I said. "You can use vacation."

"I don't have enough vacation days to -"

"You're taking the week off." My voice was irate.

She immediately leaned back and stared into her coffee mug. I sighed inwardly. I was trying to be nice, to be "gentle" like Mason suggested by giving her time off, and I was already fucking it up.

"Sweetheart," Mason said, "you deserve to take

the week off. You need some rest and, besides, you don't have any other clothes. You need to go shopping before you can come back to work."

She pulled self-consciously at her too-big top and skirt. "I should have packed some clothes but I – I just wanted to leave, and I hate my clothes." She said the last in a defiant little mutter.

"We hate your clothes too," I said.

"Oh my God," Mason said. "Dane, try and -"

He was interrupted by Naomi's adorable laugh. "My mother made them for me, and she hates that I'm fat, so she made my clothes really big to shame me."

"You're not fat," I said. "You're beautiful and I love your curves."

She blushed and took another sip of coffee. "Thank you for saying that."

"It's true. So, you need to buy some new clothes then?"

"Yes. Jemma at work asked me to go shopping with her on Saturday. I was going to say no because of my father but now I don't have to say no."

"No, baby, you don't," I said. "You can do whatever you want. In fact, I'll let Jemma know she has the day off as well. You two can go shopping today instead of waiting until Saturday."

"Oh, that's okay," she said. "I can pick up a few things this morning and then go shopping on Saturday. I have to go to my parents' place today anyway and -"

"What?" I shouted. I shouldn't have shouted but even just the idea of Naomi going anywhere near her father made my stomach twist.

Naomi's hands were clamped around her mug, her face pale and troubled. I was fucking this up so bad.

Mason stroked her arm. "Naomi, you can't go to your parents' house."

"I have to," she said.

"No, you don't." My voice was still too loud, too hard and angry, and I tried to soften it. "Baby, you can't go back there."

"I need my car," she said. "I left it there and I need it to get to work."

"You don't need a car," I said. "I'll drive you to work and anywhere else you need to go."

Little frown lines appeared on her forehead. "I need my car."

I realized what an idiot I was being. Naomi had spent her entire life being controlled by her father and even though I had the best of intentions, I was doing the same thing.

"You're right. Of course you need a car. I'll buy you a new one tomorrow," I said.

She gaped at me. "No, you're not."

Before I could argue, Mason said, "Sweetheart, Dane and I will take care of getting your car from your parents, okay?"

"You've already done enough for me," she said.

"We want to help you," Mason said. "Now, let's get some breakfast into you and then we'll go to the office and ask Jemma to go shopping with you today. All right?"

"All right," she said quietly.

Mason stood and kissed her on the forehead

before moving to the fridge. Unable to resist touching her, I reached across the table and took her hand. She smiled at me and even squeezed my hand a little, and my fucking heart immediately started racing like I was running a marathon. God, I was in so much trouble.

"You're safe with us, Naomi," I said. "I promise you."

Chapter Five

Naomi

"Okay, so exactly how controlling was your father that you just left without any clothes or anything?" Jemma parked her car in the north end of the mall parking lot.

"Pretty controlling," I admitted. "He made me give him my paycheque and I was only able to keep a little for myself. He didn't really let me have any friends and he told me what I could and couldn't wear. It's why I wear such terrible clothes and put my makeup on in the car. He joined a religious cult years ago and dragged me and my mom and my sister into it. I finally had enough when he tried to get me to marry a guy who was, like, thirty years my senior."

"Holy shit!" Jemma said. "That's fucking crazy, Naomi."

"I know."

"So, you left your house, realized you didn't have anywhere to go and went to the office?"

"Yes," I said. "I thought maybe I could just sleep on the couch in the staff room for the night and come up with a plan in the morning but Mr. Wilson, uh, Dane, came back to the office too and caught me sleeping on the couch."

I tried to keep my hands from twisting in my lap. I was a terrible liar and I felt really guilty for lying to Jemma, but I couldn't tell her the truth. I couldn't. If she knew that my boss and his best friend had bought me from my father, I would die of shame. Jemma seemed kind and sweet, but I didn't know her that well. What if she told everyone else at the office that Dane basically owned me now?

"It's really nice of Mr. Wilson to let you stay at his place," Jemma said.

"Uh, yes, it is. He has a really big house so, um, you know…"

"He likes you," Jemma said.

"No, he doesn't."

"Bullshit," she scoffed. "I saw the way he was looking at you this morning. Hell, I can't believe I didn't see it before this. Not to mention, he's letting you live at his house, he gave you the rest of the week off, and he practically demanded that I take the day off to go shopping with you. Your boss has it bad for you, sweetie, which means that Mason Shaw has it bad for you too."

I turned bright red and stared out the window of the car. "You're wrong. Dane just feels sorry for me, that's all. He would do the same for you or any other employee in the office. He's, uh, a really nice man."

Probably would have been better if I could have said it with more conviction. It wasn't that I didn't think Dane was a nice man, it was just that he made me so nervous. I hated that he made me anxious, but I didn't know how to fix it.

"I don't think he would," Jemma said. "Anyway, we're not here to argue about whether your boss wants to bang your brains out or not. We're here to get you some clothes that show off your kick-ass curves. But if things do go weird with living at Mr. Wilson's house, I rent a room in a house full of college kids that you can crash in. They party every goddamn night, you'll have to share a bed with me and a bathroom with about ten other people, but it's there if you need it."

"Thank you, but I'm good for now," I said. "Now that I can keep my entire paycheque, it shouldn't take me too much longer to save up for my own place."

Jemma smiled at me. "Well, as much as I hate the circumstances, I'll admit I'm kind of enjoying having a day off from work to go shopping with you. I've been dying to do a makeover on you since the first day I started. No offense, girl, but your clothes aren't great."

"I know, but I'm going to change that. I'm going to," I hesitated, "start living life to the fullest."

"Well," Jemma eyed my breasts critically, "I think living life to the fullest means wearing a bra that hikes your boobs up to where God intended so let's hit the lingerie store first."

ॐ ॐ

"I really shouldn't," I said.

"Why not?" Jemma opened the trunk to her car. It was nearly six hours later, and we were both laden down with bags. I hadn't actually bought that many new clothes. I didn't have a lot of cash, and I wasn't sure what Dane would be charging me for rent and groceries, so I hadn't wanted to spend too much money. But after we picked up a few new work outfits and casual outfits for me, we finished up Jemma's birthday shopping. It was fun to go shopping with her. I almost felt like a normal person. I was just a regular woman out with a friend and shopping for some new lingerie to wear for her boyfriend.

Don't you mean boss and his best friend?

I put the bags in the trunk and Jemma slammed it shut.

"I don't think Dane would like it if I went to a party with a bunch of college students," I said.

Jemma frowned at me. "He's not your boyfriend, and he's only your boss during working hours. It's nice of him to give you a place to stay but that doesn't give him the right to tell you what to do."

"He doesn't," I said immediately. "He wouldn't. I just…"

Part of me wanted to go to the party with Jemma. I had never gone to a party before, never drank alcohol or flirted with men. I wanted to try all of those things, so why was I hesitating?

Because you know what you really want is to

drink alcohol and flirt with Dane and Mason.

My inner voice was really starting to get on my nerves. Even if Dane and Mason were crazy or weird enough to actually still want me, my first time couldn't be with two men. Normal women didn't do stuff like that, and I desperately wanted to be normal.

"It's just a party," Jemma said encouragingly. "It's at the house I live in for goodness sake and I know most of the people going to the party. They're all good people, I promise. You said you wanted to live life to the fullest, right? This is the perfect opportunity to go to a party for the first time. I won't let anything bad happen to you, I promise. I have to work in the morning so it's not like I'm going to get crazy tonight."

She put her arm around my shoulders and gave me a quick squeeze. "You can even try a couple drinks if you want and just crash in my room with me tonight."

"I'll do it," I said.

"That's my girl!" Jemma said. "C'mon, we'll stop and have a quick bite to eat – my treat – and then we'll head back to my place to get ready for the party. You're going to be popular with the guys, honey, I promise."

"I don't know how to flirt," I said.

"I'll give you some pointers over dinner," she said with a careless wave of her hand. "Let's go"

"I just need to give Dane a quick call." I pulled my cell phone from my purse. There were three missed calls from my mother, but I didn't feel even a twinge of guilt. She had gone along with my father's plan to sell me to the horrible Deacon Dennison and I had nothing left to say to her.

"He's not your boyfriend," Jemma reminded me.

"I know," I said, "but he was expecting me back for dinner and it would be rude not to let him know I had a change in plans. It'll take me one minute to call him."

"All right, but don't let him talk you out of it," Jemma said.

"Why would he?"

She rolled her eyes. "It's almost adorable how clueless you are to the fact that your boss wants to bend you over his desk and fuck you silly."

I turned scarlet and scowled at her. She laughed and climbed into the car. "Go on. Give Mr. Wilson a call while we're driving to the restaurant. Let's see what he says about you going off to party with a bunch of college boys."

Mason

When Dane's cell phone rang, I snagged it from his desk. I didn't recognize the number. "Dane, your phone's ringing."

"Answer it," he shouted. He was sitting outside his office at Naomi's desk, searching her computer for a file. I was about to suggest he either give up or give Naomi a quick call.

I hit the answer button. "Good afternoon, Mason Shaw speaking."

"Mason?" Naomi's soft voice held surprise.

"Why are you answering Dane's phone?"

"Hi!" I sounded like an overexcited schoolboy and I cringed. I had a feeling I was on the verge of falling for Naomi just as hard as Dane had.

"Hi," she said. "Is Dane okay?"

"He's fine," I said. "Just looking for the Garret file on your computer. Any idea off the top of your head where it is?"

"Yes, it's under the new proposals folder."

"Perfect, thanks, sweetheart. How was your day of shopping?"

"Um, it was really good. I got some new clothes. Clothes that fit." Her voice turned shy. "Jemma says they look really good on me."

"I can't wait to see them tonight," I said. If my growing cock was any indication, I also couldn't wait to see her *out* of those new clothes.

"Uh, that's actually why I'm calling. Jemma invited me to go to a party at her house tonight and I said yes."

My stomach dropped. I wanted to immediately drive to the mall and snatch Naomi away from Jemma. Instead I said, "That sounds like fun."

"Yeah, I think it will be," she said. "I might just crash at Jemma's tonight too. Just because, you know, we might have a couple of drinks."

Every part of me wanted to tell her no. Tell her that she wasn't allowed to go to a party without us, and she certainly wasn't allowed to drink alcohol when we weren't around.

"Have you tried alcohol before?" I asked.

"No."

"Don't have more than one or two drinks," I

said. I sounded as harsh as Dane, but I couldn't help myself. The thought of Naomi being drunk around other guys made my blood boil. What if they took advantage of her?

"I won't," she said. "I just want to try it."

I bit back my urge to beg her to just come home with us. I couldn't do that to her. "Okay, well, have fun and be safe. If you want to come home, just call us and we'll come and get you. It doesn't matter what time."

I winced. Fuck, now I sounded like a goddamn parent, but I couldn't seem to stop. "Do you have my cell number?"

"No, but I have Dane's," she said.

"I'll text you mine. Make sure you add it to your contacts."

"Okay," she said. "I'd better go. Jemma and I are going out for dinner and we're almost at the restaurant."

"Sure," I said. "Have fun, sweetheart. I mean that."

"Thanks," she said. "I'll see you tomorrow."

I wondered if it was disappointment I heard in her voice. I ended the call and set Dane's phone on the desk as he stalked back into his office.

"I can't find the fucking file," he said. "I'm going to have to call Naomi."

"It's under 'new proposals'," I said. "That was Naomi calling."

"What?" Dane's gaze flickered to his cell phone. "Why didn't you let me talk to her?"

He grabbed his phone and stared at it like he thought Naomi might still be on the line. I arched my eyebrows at him, and he actually blushed. "Don't say it, Mason. I know I sound like an idiot."

"No, you sound like a man in love," I said.

He didn't reply and I said, "Holy fuck, you are in love with her."

"Maybe I am," he said. "I can't stop thinking about her, worrying about her, wishing she was safe by my side every fucking minute of the day."

"Never took you for the insta-love type," I said with a grin. "Always thought that would be me."

"You're in love with her too," Dane said. "You just haven't figured it out yet."

I shrugged and Dane glanced at his phone again. "Is she on her way back to the office?"

"No, she's going to a party at Jemma's house tonight."

"The fuck she is!" Dane said. "Why the fuck did you tell her she could go?"

"Because she's a grown woman and can make her own decisions," I said.

Dane slammed his office door shut. "I'm going to kill you, Mason. Do you know where Jemma lives?"

"No."

"She lives in a fucking house full of goddamn college kids!"

"How do you know that?"

He stalked back and forth. "I overheard her talking in the staff room one day. We can't let Naomi be at a party with a bunch of drunk frat guys. I'm not going to let some hotheaded, stupid college kid take what's mine!"

"It's not our decision," I said patiently even

though my insides were churning. If Dane even suspected that I wanted to bring Naomi back to our home and never let her leave, he'd be doing everything in his power to convince me it was a damn fine idea. "Dane, just listen to me for a minute. Naomi is twenty-three years old. Both of us are almost a decade older than her. We've spent the last eight years building this company from the ground up, making a shit load of money and fucking any woman who was into us. We've been," I paused, "living our lives exactly the way we want to. Naomi has spent her entire life being told what to do and when to do it. For the first time in her life, she has freedom. If we try and take that away from her, she's going to resent us or hate us."

"I just want to keep her safe," Dane said.

"I know, I do too. But we can't do that by telling her how to live her life. Naomi's a smart woman. She won't do anything reckless or crazy."

"You don't know that," Dane said morosely. "She might."

"She won't." I hesitated and then said, "I thought about what you said this morning and I think you're right, we should talk to her. We'll tell her what we're like in bed and let her decide if that's too…controlling for her. But if she says no -"

"We'll just have vanilla sex with her," Dane said.

"Eventually that won't be enough for me," I said, "and if you're honest with yourself, it won't be enough for you either. If she's hesitant about us dominating her, then yes, we can suggest vanilla to begin with. But she needs to know that we'll want it to evolve into more than just that. And you need to be prepared that she may just say no to all of it."

"She wants both of us," Dane said stubbornly.

"She does, but she was in a religious cult for most of her life that would have convinced her fucking two guys at once is a sin," I said. "Hell, you saw how she was after we made her cum. She was freaked out."

Dane dropped into his office chair before rubbing at his forehead. "If she says no, I'll lose my goddamn mind, Mason."

"Just stay calm when we talk to her," I said. "Give her plenty of space and don't expect her to answer right away. She's going to need some time to think about it."

"Yeah, I know," Dane grunted.

I clapped him on the back before heading for the door. "I've got some errands to run after work. I'll see you at home."

Chapter Six

Naomi

I had made a mistake. I should never have come to the party. Should never have tried to be normal. I wasn't normal and I was a fool to think that I ever could be. My father had done too much damage.

I took a deep breath and tried to calm my racing heart. It was hot in the house, but I didn't think that was why I was so sweaty, and the one beer and one shot I had tried shouldn't have made me this nauseous. I couldn't catch my breath and my chest was too tight. There were so many people and after years of spending most of my time with just my parents and my sister, being around this many people made me anxious and unsettled.

Jemma was standing next to me, and I tried to smile at her when she nudged me. "Isn't this great?"

"Yeah, it's really great," I said.

She glanced at my half-full beer. "What do you

think of the beer?"

"Um, it's good."

She laughed. "I doubt that. I think Rick is making Caesars over at the bar. Do you want me to grab one for you? You might like it."

"No, I don't think so." I leaned against the wall and tried not to notice the way everyone was standing too close. The house was packed full of drunk college students and try as I might, I didn't fit in with them. I might have been around their age, but we had nothing else in common. My education was limited to graduating high school and even then, my mother had homeschooled me.

Even though Jemma had made sure to stay with me the entire night and was sweet and kind in introducing me to everyone who came up to us, I was an outcast. Jemma flirted and giggled and acted normal with the guys who approached us, but I could barely work up the nerve to talk to them. They all seemed too young, too immature, and not...

Not Dane or Mason.

Just thinking their names eased some of the pressure in my chest. I wished to God I had told Jemma no and gone home to their house. If I had done that, then maybe I wouldn't be struggling to breathe, wouldn't have this sharp, stabbing pain in my chest. Fresh fear flooded through me. Was I having a heart attack?

My stomach churned, my mouth watered, and I knew I was going to throw up. I grabbed Jemma's arm. "Bathroom," I croaked, "where is it?"

"Honey, are you okay? You're really pale,"

Jemma said.

"Bathroom," I croaked again.

"Down that hallway, second door on the left," she said.

I pushed through the crowd of people as the pain in my chest deepened and my urge to vomit grew stronger. I threw my hand over my mouth and bolted down the hallway. I grabbed the door handle and pushed. To my surprise and relief, the room was empty. I slipped into the room, slamming the door and locking it before dropping to my knees in front of the toilet and vomiting.

Someone pounded on the door and then Jemma's voice said, "Naomi? Honey, let me in."

I sat back, wiping my face with a shaking hand. I was still holding my beer in the other hand and I set it on the floor before flushing the toilet. My legs were shaking and weak, and I was so ashamed I couldn't stop the tears. I was a freak and now Jemma and everyone at this stupid party knew it.

Poor little freak girl who spent her life in a cult.

I rubbed at my chest and ignored Jemma's repeated knocking and pleading to unlock the door. I wanted Mason and Dane with a singlemindedness that scared me in its ferocity. I reached for my phone in my pocket before hesitating. I couldn't call them. I couldn't let them see how pathetic I was.

As Jemma continued to knock, I buried my face in my hands and tried to ignore both Jemma and the pain in my chest. After only a few minutes, Jemma stopped knocking but I continued to sit on the floor. I couldn't go back out there with all those people, I just couldn't.

It wasn't sure how much time passed, but the pain in my chest was starting to ease a little and it seemed a bit easier to breathe. I took an experimental deep breath that turned into a squeak of surprise when there was a knock on the door.

"Naomi? Sweetheart, let me in."

My heart kicked up a notch and I took a few shallow breaths. What was Mason doing here? I started to climb to my feet, tears already sliding down my face, before I slumped to the floor again. I couldn't let him see me like this. I would die of shame.

"Naomi. Open the door, please."

"Go away," I said. "Leave me alone, Mason."

"Please open the door," Mason said. "I just want to talk to you."

"No!" I screamed. I was starting to feel hysterical and my ability to breathe normally was all but lost. "Go away! I – I'm fine. Okay? I'm perfectly fine."

"Sweetheart -"

"Go away!"

"Naomi, unlock the door right now."

The demand in Dane's deep voice had me on my feet and staggering to the door immediately. I hesitated and as if he sensed it, Dane said, "Now, Naomi. Or I'll break it down."

I unlocked the door and backed away as it opened. Mason rushed in, followed closely by Dane and Jemma. I rubbed away the tears on my cheeks. "What are you doing here?"

"I called Mr. Wilson," Jemma said as Mason

approached me like I was a timid deer. "I was worried about you, honey."

"I'm fine," I lied. "Just a little overwhelmed and…"

My voice died as I took a good look at Dane. Anger was stamped all over his face and my fragile control broke at the thought that he might be angry with me. I burst into tears and covered my face with my hands.

"Shh, sweetheart. It's okay." Mason pulled me into his embrace and kissed my forehead. "Let's get you home."

"D-d-do you even want me there?"

"Of course, we do." Mason put his arm around me and led me toward the door.

Still crying, I said, "Jemma, I – I'm sorry."

"No, I'm sorry," she said. "I think the party was a bit too much for you and I should have known that."

"It's not your fault," I said as Mason guided me out of the bathroom. There were too many people standing in the hallway, and I froze, my heart beating hard and fast. "Mason, too many – I can't."

"Move!" Dane's angry voice echoed down the hallway. "All of you assholes get the fuck out of here."

"Jesus, dude. Chill out," one of the guys said. He rolled his eyes but followed the others as they filed out of the hallway.

I didn't object when Mason picked me up and carried me down the hallway toward the front door. Dane pushed in front of us and I stared at his broad back before burying my face in Mason's neck. I didn't want to see the looks on the party-goer's faces as I was carried out like a wailing baby, but I didn't want Mason to put me down either.

"The new clothes she bought are still in the trunk of my car," Jemma said.

"Come outside with us and Dane will get them," Mason said.

I lifted my head when I felt the cold air. "I'm sorry, Mason."

"It's fine," he said soothingly as he carried me to the car. "It's fine, sweetheart. Let's go home."

∫ ∫

Naomi

I stood timidly in the hallway outside of the living room of Dane's home. Two hours and one hot shower later and I was feeling better.

Embarrassed and ashamed, but better.

I took a deep breath, cinched my robe a little tighter around my waist, and walked into the living room. It was only Mason sitting on the couch, staring blankly at the TV, and some of my tension eased a little. I didn't want to face Dane yet. I knew he was angry with me and I wasn't ready to see his anger or his disappointment.

"Mason?" I almost whispered.

He shut the TV off and stood up. "Sweetheart? How do you feel now?"

"Better," I said. "I had a shower and I... I'm really sorry."

"You don't have to apologize," he said. "Come sit on the couch with me."

I took his hand when he held it out to me, and we sat down on the couch. He cuddled me for a few minutes before stroking the braid that was wound around my head.

"Where's Dane?" I asked.

"He's around," Mason said. "Do you want something to eat?"

"No," I said. "I ate dinner with Jemma. Are you – will you make me leave in the morning?"

"What?" Mason turned my face toward his. "No, we're not making you leave, Naomi. Not unless you want to."

"I don't," I said, "but I know Dane is angry with me and -"

"He's not angry," Mason said. "He's worried about you, just like I am. He just doesn't control his emotions as well as I do."

I studied him, and he leaned forward and pressed a kiss against my mouth. "We want you to have fun and make friends and enjoy new experiences, Naomi. But we also want you to be safe."

"Kiss me again," I whispered.

He hesitated and I said, "Please kiss me, Mason. I need you."

He cupped my face and kissed me gently. I opened my mouth and moaned when he licked my upper lip before sliding his tongue into my mouth.

When he pulled away, I protested loudly and he said, "Sweetheart, you're upset and tired and -"

"I'm not." Feeling bold and needy, I cupped his face and kissed him hard. When his lips parted, I pushed my tongue into his mouth and moaned when he sucked on my tongue.

I didn't object when he pushed me onto my back on the couch and hovered over me. He cupped my breast through my robe and my nightgown and squeezed.

"You taste so good," he groaned against my mouth.

"So do you," I whispered.

He teased my nipple through the silk fabric, and I cried out again before clutching at his waist and kissing him frantically. I had no idea how much time passed and didn't care. I was addicted to Mason's kisses and wanted more.

I didn't realize I was rubbing myself against his crotch until he cupped my hip and whispered, "Sweetheart, stop."

"I'm sorry." I suddenly realized how slutty I looked. Mason's hard body was pressing me deep into the couch, my new robe and nightgown had ridden up until they barely covered my crotch and the front of the robe gaped open, giving Mason ample access to my silk-covered breasts.

"You don't have to be sorry." He sat up and I straightened my clothes and sat up beside him.

He rubbed my bare knee. "I want you very much, Naomi."

"I – I want you too," I said. "We don't have to stop."

He smiled ruefully. "We do. I'll end up taking your virginity right here on the couch if we don't."

Heat flooded through me. "I'm good with that."

He gave me a look of fierce desire before shaking his head. "No, sweetheart. I can't."

"I want you to have it."

"Believe me, there is nothing I would love more but it isn't my gift to take."

"What do you mean?" I said.

"Dane, sweetheart. Dane wants to be your first and I've agreed to it."

"But what if I don't want him to take it?"

"Then he won't," Mason said.

"So, you will?"

"No."

"So, I'll just be a virgin forever?" Frustration had replaced the heat.

He smiled. "I doubt that. You have no idea how many men would kill to be between those smooth thighs of yours."

His smile faded and he pulled me into his embrace before kissing me. "You should give it to Dane, sweet one. He understands the importance of it."

"He frightens me," I said.

"Why?"

"Well, because he's mean and -"

"He isn't mean. He's strict but can you really say he's mean?" Mason said. "Has he ever been cruel to you at work?"

"Well, no," I admitted. "But he's not," I grasped for the word, "gentle, like you are. He – he doesn't ask me to do things like you do, he tells me to do them and I don't like that."

"Don't you?" Mason said.

"No, I…"

Mason waited patiently while I thought it over. Did I like it? I thought back to that moment in his office when Dane had ordered me to remove my bra, when he had kissed me like he owned my mouth, and a shudder of desire went through me.

"I'm not sure," I said.

"Listen carefully to me, Naomi." Mason cupped my face. "Dane would never hurt you. He would never do anything you didn't want him to do. Do you understand?"

I nodded, and he stroked the curve of my jaw with his thumb. "It's fucking killing him that you're afraid of him. I'm not asking you to pretend you're not afraid – if you are, you are and that's something Dane needs to fix – but I am asking you to give him a chance. Let him show you that he would die before he hurt you. Will you give him that chance?"

"I'll try," I said.

"Good girl." He kissed me on the mouth, and I pressed myself eagerly against him as he deepened the kiss.

His hand cupped my breast again and he squeezed and kneaded it until I was moaning. He stiffened when I pressed my hand against the bulge in his jeans.

"Mason?" I breathed against his mouth.

"Yeah?"

"I've never seen a penis before."

He grinned and I blushed when he said, "Sweetheart, call it a cock."

I cleared my throat. "Cock. I've never seen a cock before."

Another look of intense desire flashed across his face and his hand tightened on my breast until I gasped.

"You have no idea what it does to me to hear you say cock," he muttered. "Swear to God, I'll have your sweet mouth talking dirty in no time."

I blushed again. "I wouldn't know what to say."

"I'll teach you, don't worry," he said with a wicked grin. "You honestly have never seen one before?"

I shook my head and he frowned at me. "You never once googled it?"

"My father had blocks on the internet. I've only looked at religious websites," I said.

A look of disgust crossed his face and I said, "I'm sorry."

"Don't apologize," he said. "It's not your fault. Now, do you want to see my cock?"

I nodded, and he brushed his hand over the braid wound around my head. "Say it, sweetheart."

"I want to see your cock," I said.

"See, talking dirty already." He unbuttoned and unzipped his jeans before tugging the front of his briefs down. His cock sprang free and I stared curiously at it. It was long and thick looking, and the head was leaking a clear fluid. I wondered briefly if he was considered big. It stood straight up from its nest of blond pubic hair and I gave Mason a tentative look.

"May I touch it?"

"Yes, sweetheart, you may," he said.

I wrapped my fingers around the shaft, my eyes widening at how warm and velvety-soft the skin was. It was as hard as steel beneath that velvet skin, and I stroked it lightly, stopping when Mason groaned.

"Does that hurt?"

"Fuck no," he said. "Rub faster."

I did what he asked, watching in fascination as more liquid dripped from the slit in the head. I tried tightening my grip and moving my hand in long, slow, strokes, smiling delightedly when Mason groaned, and his hips bucked.

"Does that feel good?"

"You have no fucking idea how good it feels," he said. "Keep going, sweetheart. Rub my cock with your soft hand."

I pulled and tugged, switching my gaze between Mason's cock and his face. I didn't know what I liked more – the look of intensity on his face or the way his cock felt in my hand.

Dane walked into the room, stopping briefly when he saw us. My hand tightened on Mason's cock until he groaned, and I started to release him.

"No," Mason ground out. His hand covered mine and kept it on his cock. "Don't stop, sweetheart."

Licking my lips nervously, I continued to stroke his cock as Dane sat down on the other end of the couch. He watched me touch Mason's cock and I dropped my eyes to avoid his gaze. My breath hitched in my throat when I saw the bulge in Dane's pants.

"You okay?" Mason said.

"Yeah," Dane said.

Mason cupped my head and kissed me on the mouth. "Why don't you scoot over to Dane and let him kiss your sweet mouth. I bet it would make him feel better."

I stared uncertainly at Mason and he said, "Go on, sweetheart," before taking my hand off his dick and kissing the palm of it. I chewed on my bottom lip before sliding across the couch toward Dane.

Dane

I tried to keep the look of need off my face when Naomi stared uncertainly at Mason.

"Go on, sweetheart," he coaxed before removing her hand from his dick and kissing her palm.

Part of me was embarrassed that Mason had to ask Naomi to go near me, but a larger, deeper part of me was so desperate to feel her soft mouth and body that it eclipsed my shame.

Naomi bit at her lip before sliding her curvy body closer to mine. "Hi, Dane."

"Hey," I grunted. I put my arm across the back of the couch, silently encouraging her to move closer, and she hesitated before curling against my side.

"I'm sorry about what happened earlier."

"Do you feel better?"

"Yes," she whispered.

I stared at her lush mouth as she licked her lips. I could barely stop my groan at the sight of her little pink tongue. She lifted her head and pressed her mouth tentatively against mine. I forced myself to kiss her gently, even though every part of me was screaming to possess her. To show her she was ours and always would be.

I sucked on her bottom lip before tracing her upper lip with my tongue. She moaned and pressed a little closer as she parted her lips. I took advantage of her silent invitation, slipping my tongue into her mouth to lick at her inner cheeks and tongue. She squirmed against me, and I wrapped my arms around her and hoisted her onto my lap until she was straddling me. I pressed my erection against her as I cupped her face and deepened the kiss.

I nipped at her bottom lip, soothing the slight sting with my tongue, and groaned when she pressed her breasts against my chest. I continued to kiss her, taking what was mine with hard licks and nips until her pelvis was pressing rhythmically against my crotch.

Her arms were folded across her torso and I said, "Move your arms, baby."

She moved her arms immediately and my dick throbbed at how quickly she obeyed. I untied her robe and pushed it off her body. Her nipples were hard against her silk nightgown and I took it as a good sign when she didn't immediately cover her breasts with her arms. I traced the pale pink silk of her nightgown.

"This is very pretty," I said.

She ducked her head and stared at my chest. "Thank you." She gave me a painfully shy look before whispering, "The panties match."

"Let me see. Stand up, baby."

She stood and I leaned forward and lifted her nightgown up. She didn't resist when I tugged on the waistband of her pretty, pink panties. My nostrils flared as I stared at her and Mason made a soft groan and gripped his cock. He rubbed hard as Naomi stared tentatively at me.

"Is it okay?"

"Baby, you look so fucking hot, I'm about to explode in my pants," I said. "Come back here."

Another flare of lust when she obeyed me. I resisted the urge to send Mason to the bedroom for the collar and cuffs. God, what it would fucking do to me to see that leather collar around her throat. To cuff her to the headboard, blindfold her, and taste and tease her until she was begging for mercy.

I reined myself in as Naomi's soft weight settled onto my thighs. I traced my finger across the swell of her breasts before grabbing the hem of her nightgown.

"Arms up, baby."

Another throb in my dick when she lifted her arms without question. I pulled her nightgown over her head and dropped it to the floor. Her breasts were incredible, and I could barely stop from rubbing my cock against her. Instead, I traced my fingers over her ribcage and smiled when her pale skin broke out in goosebumps.

"You have the prettiest tits I've ever seen," I said.

"Th-thank you," she said.

Mason stood and she stiffened a little when he moved behind her. "Shh, sweetheart. You don't have to be nervous."

He tugged on her arms until she rose up off my lap, her knees digging into the couch cushion on either side of my thighs. I missed her soft weight, but the new position put her beautiful breasts directly in front of my face.

I ran my thumbs over her nipples before pinching and tugging on them. She moaned as her back arched and I squeezed a little harder. I wanted to see what her tolerance level was, and, to my delight, the slight pain seemed to increase her excitement.

Mason stroked her back before kissing the curve of her shoulder. Both of us were still fully clothed and there was something darkly exciting about having Naomi almost naked between us.

I leaned forward and tasted her nipples for the first time. They beaded into little points in my mouth and I teased them with my tongue before giving one a hard nip with my teeth. She gasped, her entire body jerking, and stared wide-eyed at me as I licked and soothed her nipple.

"I'm sorry. Did that hurt, baby?"

"A little," she whispered. "I – I kind of liked it though."

Her confession made my hips buck against her and she made another little gasp as Mason lifted her arms and draped them around his neck. Her eyes widened, obviously Mason was rubbing his dick against her ass, but she didn't resist when he turned her face toward him and kissed her.

"Keep your arms around my neck," Mason said when he released her mouth. "If you move them, I'll spank you, sweetheart. Do you understand?"

I glared at him. We hadn't talked to Naomi about our tastes in bed and Mason would scare the living daylights out of her with his threat of spanking. To my surprise, a little flush of heat brightened her cheeks and she gave him a sweetly submissive look.

"Would you really spank me?"

Mason nodded and squeezed her ass. "Yes, sweetheart, I really would."

"But not if you're a good girl," I said. I licked between her large breasts and she made a soft mewling noise of pleasure. "Will you be our good girl, Naomi?"

"Yes," she gasped.

"Say it," I demanded.

"I'll be your good girl, Dane."

I smiled my satisfaction as Mason cupped her breasts and she leaned back against his chest. I quickly unbuttoned my pants and pulled my cock out.

"It's thicker," she said.

I grinned at Mason who rolled his eyes and Naomi's mouth pursed into a little 'o'. "I'm sorry. I didn't mean to – I mean, I don't care that -"

"Relax, sweetheart." Mason squeezed her breasts. "I'm not the kind of guy who worries about size."

She stared worriedly at him. "I like yours, Mason."

He laughed. "It likes you too, sweetheart."

She still looked worried. He kissed her hard, squeezing and kneading her tits until she was moaning and rubbing against him. I pressed my fingers against her silk-covered pussy, rubbing at her clit through the fabric until a wet spot appeared.

"Oh," she cried breathlessly, her hips flexing against my fingers, "oh, that feels so good."

Mason reached for the waistband of her panties and pulled them down her thighs. "Show Dane your pretty little pussy, sweetheart."

We helped ease her panties past her knees and down her legs. Mason dropped them to the floor. He pulled her ass cheeks apart and nestled his cock between them. He rubbed up and down as my gaze dropped to her pussy. It was covered in dark curls and she blushed again.

"I – I was thinking I would make an appointment for waxing. I've never -"

"No," I said. "No one sees your pussy but us. If you decide you want to wax it, we'll do it."

"You know how to do that?" she said.

I touched the dark curls with my fingers. "Yes."

Her pussy was dripping wet and I pushed my index finger between her wet lips and rubbed her swollen clit. She moaned, her hips thrusting forward, and precum leaked from my dick. God, I wanted to fuck her so badly.

I cupped her pale thighs – I had never seen anyone with such perfect, pale skin in my life – and tugged her forward until her pussy brushed against the head of my cock. I groaned and she gasped when Mason stepped forward between my legs and rubbed his dick between her ass cheeks again.

I pushed my cock between her wet pussy lips and both Mason and I moved her up and down. I watched my cock sliding back and forth, her lips clinging to its thick length. She made a little gasp of need every time the head of my cock bumped against her clit that set my skin on fire with lust.

"Oh, oh, please," she whimpered.

I grabbed my cock and rubbed it even harder against her. I couldn't resist sliding the head of it to her wet hole and probing gently.

"Dane," Mason said, "she's not ready."

"I know," I said through gritted teeth before moving my dick back to her clit.

"I'm ready," Naomi said in a soft whimper. "Please, Dane. I'm ready."

"You're not, sweetheart," Mason said.

She glared at him before turning her gaze to me. "Please, Dane?"

Her sweet pleading tone just about did me in. I stared at Mason who shook his head again. "No, you know she isn't."

"Stop saying that," Naomi said. "I'm ready."

I gritted my teeth and rubbed my cock back and forth over her clit. "Not this time, baby. But soon."

"Do you promise?" she moaned.

"Yes," I said. "I'll fuck you soon."

My cock was already drenched in her juices and I slid it up and down as she cried out with pleasure. Mason was rubbing his dick frantically between her ass cheeks and he pinched her nipples hard as I pressed the head of my cock against her clit. Her loud moans and the way she was rubbing herself against my dick made my balls tighten painfully.

"Mason," I gritted out, "I'm fucking close."

"Me too," he gasped.

He squeezed Naomi's tits as I rubbed my cock back and forth over her clit. "Naomi, cum for us," Mason said.

She moaned and her eyelids fluttered open. She stared at me and I pushed my fingers past my cock and rubbed her clit before pinching it.

"Oh my God!" she shouted.

"Cum right now, Naomi," I said. I pinched her clit again just as Mason pinched her nipples. She screamed, arched her back, and climaxed with another loud scream. Her beautiful body tensed before her pelvis rocked back and forth wildly. Warm liquid covered my cock and I was only vaguely aware of Mason's low groan of pleasure. I fisted my cock frantically, staring at Naomi's wet pussy. I wanted to rub my dick against her pussy again, but I didn't trust myself not to just thrust deep into her wet pussy and make her mine forever. Her body was being pushed forward by the frantic rutting of Mason's cock between her ass cheeks. He groaned again before grabbing her hips and holding tightly as he came all over her ass and back.

She cried out at the unexpected wetness, and I groaned and aimed my dick at her pussy before rubbing hard. My orgasm hit me hard and fast and I jerked off furiously, my cum splattering over her pussy and lower belly. When the last of my cum covered her pale flesh, I collapsed against the couch, breathing harshly as Mason held Naomi in a tight grip.

"You okay, sweetheart?" he murmured into her ear as she swayed in his arms. Her eyes were closed and the look of bliss on her face made me grin.

"I'm better than okay," she said.

"Good. Let's get you into bed," Mason said.

"Will you guys come with me?" she asked without opening her eyes.

My goddamn dick actually twitched at the thought of being in her bed, but Mason shook his head. "No, sweetheart. You need to get some rest and we'll talk in the morning."

She pouted adorably as Mason helped her slide off my lap. I stood – fuck, my own legs were feeling decidedly rubbery – and kissed her pouting mouth. She gave me her first smile that wasn't tinged with anxiety and my chest tightened.

"Thank you, Dane."

"You're welcome, baby," I said as she yawned.

"Thank you, Mason."

"Anytime, sweetheart," he said.

I picked up her robe and Mason helped her into it before putting his arm around her waist. "Let's get you tucked into bed." He glanced at me. "Are you coming with us?"

I shook my head. If I even took one step into Naomi's bedroom, I'd have her on her back in the bed, legs spread wide, and fucking her until she was screaming my name. My dick twitched again, and Mason glanced at it before rolling his eyes.

I cleared my throat and tucked my hardening dick back into my pants. "Good night, Naomi."

"Good night, Dane," she said sleepily as Mason led her out of the living room.

Chapter Seven

Naomi

I brushed my hair with long, smooth strokes, admiring how shiny it was in the light from the early morning sun. I was sitting on my bed and I threaded my hair through my fingers before beginning to braid it. I stopped abruptly and stared at myself in the full-length mirror that was hanging on the wall closest to me. I didn't have to braid it. I could leave it free like other women did.

Feeling a thrill at my small act of rebellion, I smoothed my hair down before dropping my damp towel and putting on my underclothes. I studied my body in the dark blue lace bra and matching panties. I'd never had anything this pretty for underwear before. I finished dressing and stared at the jeans that hugged my lower body and the bright pink top that clung to my breasts. They both looked scandalously tight to me, but Jemma had assured me they weren't. My father hadn't strictly forbidden my mother, sister and me to wear pants, but he frowned on it and made rude comments if we wore them too often. In the last ten years, I think I had worn pants three times and only once had it been jeans.

I turned and studied my ass. It looked fat to me, but Dane had said I wasn't fat. He said they loved my curves. A little shiver went down my spine. I'd been completely naked with two men last night. Two men had made me orgasm and I'd woken up this morning with their dried semen on my lower back and belly. I should have felt dirty from it, but I hadn't. I'd felt cherished and…loved almost. I made an unladylike snort. Dane and Mason didn't love me. They lusted after me but once they got what they wanted they would move on to the next woman.

But you're still going to let both of them fuck you. Maybe even at the same time. My inner voice sounded horrified.

Yes, I was. I had made my decision in the shower this morning. I wanted my virginity gone and I wanted both Mason and Dane. My desire to be normal and live the same life that everyone else did was still there but it was buried so deep under my lust for both men that I wasn't sure it would ever see the light of day again. At least not until they were finished with me.

This makes you a whore. You know that, right?

I guessed that it probably did but I couldn't bring myself to care. I had made a fool of myself trying to be normal last night. Maybe being a sweet normal girl wasn't something I could be. Other than Jemma's descriptions of her various trysts with different men, I'd never talked about sex with another woman before. But I was guessing that most women didn't get excited about the thought of having a cock in her pussy and a cock in her ass at the same time.

Jemma wanted both of them at once. She told you that.

That was true. But Jemma seemed to like sex a whole lot and she had never once mentioned a steady boyfriend. Maybe she was a whore as well.

Even just thinking about Mason and Dane fucking me together made my pussy tingle. I shifted against the bed. Already I was thinking dirty thoughts and using bad words in my head. Didn't that just prove my point that I was meant to be a whore and not a good girl?

"Whore," I whispered. "I'm a whore."

I glanced upward and when God didn't strike me dead, I said, "I'm a whore who is going to – to fuck two men at once."

Curiously enough, saying it out loud made me feel good so I said it twice more before grabbing my phone from the nightstand. It was time to go downstairs and tell Dane and Mason that I wanted to have sex with them. Heat infused my cheeks, but I tamped down my embarrassment. I didn't want to – *couldn't* - be normal. I was –

My phone rang in my hand and I almost dropped it. I stared at the number and let it ring twice more before hitting the answer button. "Hello, Mom."

"Naomi? Oh my goodness, Naomi! I've been so worried about you. Why haven't you returned my calls?"

"I've been busy," I said.

"Have you – are you okay?" she said.

"I'm fine. Why are you calling?"

My mother made an indignant sound. "Why am I calling? You're my daughter, Naomi, and two strange men just – just stole you away from us. I've been scared stiff about what's happened to you."

My laughter felt like jagged knives in my throat. "They didn't steal me, Mom. They bought me. For a hundred grand, remember?"

"Honey, I – I didn't want to do that."

"No?" I said. "But you were perfectly fine with selling me for twenty-five thousand dollars to Deacon Dennison?"

"We had no choice, honey. You – you know that."

"You had a choice!" I said. "You had a choice and you made the wrong one. I have to go."

"Naomi, wait!"

My mother was starting to cry, and a sliver of guilt trickled through me. "Mom, I'm fine. Dane and Mason are really good to me – much better than Deacon Dennison would have been. My life is better now so don't worry about me."

"I want you to come home," she whispered. "Please just come home. Those – those men can't legally keep you. There weren't any contracts signed or promises made."

"I can't come back home," I said. "Are you crazy, Mom? I can't live with Dad anymore and you shouldn't either. It's going to take me a few months to get enough money for my own place but once I do, maybe you could – I don't know – stay with me for a bit."

My anger at my mother's betrayal was disappearing under a wave of pity.

"I can't leave your father, honey," my mother said. "Please, just come home and we'll forget all about what happened."

"Until the next time he needs money and tries to sell me again," I said. "I'm not coming home, Mom. Not while he's there."

"He isn't here," she said. "So, why don't you come home, and we'll have some girl time - just you and me for a few days. By the time your father comes back, you'll see why you shouldn't have moved out."

"Where is he?" I was immediately suspicious. My father rarely travelled, and he certainly didn't travel without my mother.

"I – well, he had some business stuff to take care of in Vegas."

"Dad is in Vegas?" I said. "For business."

"Yes," she said.

"Why would he go to Vegas for business? He never travels for…

The truth hit me like a brick. "Holy shit. He's gambling the hundred thousand, isn't he?"

"Don't curse, Naomi. It isn't ladylike," my mother said automatically.

"Fuck ladylike," I spat into the phone. I ignored my mother's horrified gasp. "He's gambling with the money that Dane and Mason gave to him! He's insane."

"He – he is struggling with sin right now,

Naomi. When he finds the strength from God to -"

"He isn't going to find God in Vegas," I said. "I have to go. Please don't call me again."

"Naomi, please, I -"

I pushed the end button and stared at the screen of my cell phone. It was old and battered and the plan was under my father's name. I was surprised he hadn't cancelled it yet.

Just another way to keep his claws in you.

I suddenly tossed my cell phone into the small garbage can by the bed. I would buy a cell phone and set up an account under my own name with my next paycheque. I still needed to talk to Dane and Mason about how much my share of rent and groceries would be, but I was confident they would be okay with me possibly using rent money to get a new phone just this once.

I stared at myself in the mirror before tugging at my t-shirt. I thought I would be upset after talking to my mother but, oddly, I wasn't. In fact, it felt like a heavy weight had lifted off my shoulders. I had lost my mother but if I was being honest, I had stopped thinking of her as my mother the day she let my father send Joy away. I was free of my father for the first time and I was nearly giddy with happiness.

Smiling, I walked out of my room and ran down the stairs. I could hear Dane and Mason talking in the kitchen and my footsteps slowed when I realized they were arguing. I crept to the doorway and leaned against the wall, listening intently as they argued about whether they should fuck me or not.

ই✦ ✦ও

Mason

"Dane, we can't."

"For fuck's sake, Mason," Dane paced in the kitchen. "What the hell is wrong with you? One minute you're fine with having sex with her and the next, you're not. Didn't last night prove to you that Naomi wants to be with us? Both of us? She wanted to have sex."

I sighed and rubbed at my forehead. "She wanted to have vanilla sex with us, Dane. I'm still not sure that -"

"You were the one who threatened to spank her!" Dane snarled. "Or have you fucking forgot that?"

"No, I haven't," I said. "And that's my point. I'm not capable of doing just vanilla sex anymore. I'm dominant and so are you and trying to hide that or pretend it doesn't exist around Naomi isn't fair to any of us."

"We're not going to hide it," Dane said. "We're going to talk to her, remember?"

"She won't want that," I said. "She'll only want vanilla sex."

"Then I'll give her vanilla sex."

I sighed. "I already told you, I can't do just vanilla sex."

"I didn't say 'we'," Dane said.

"Seriously?" Hurt infused my words.

"You told me before that you would go ahead and seduce Naomi even if I didn't," Dane said.

I wanted to tell him he was a fucking asshole, but he had a point. Before I realized just how badly Naomi's father had fucked her up, I'd been more than willing to go ahead and seduce her – with or without Dane.

"She's a natural submissive," Dane said.

"Because of her father," I countered. "It isn't healthy."

"You don't know that for sure," Dane said.

My hurt turned to frustration, but Dane said with calm finality, "I'm going to fuck her, Mason. And I'll fuck her without you if I have to."

"That isn't what I want."

We both froze and then stared guiltily at Naomi standing in the doorway. She was wearing tight jeans and a shirt that hugged her tits, and my dick immediately made a bid for freedom against my zipper. For the first time ever, her hair wasn't braided, and I stared in fascination at it as she joined Dane at the coffee maker and poured herself a cup of coffee. Her hair fell to her waist and it looked shiny and so goddamn soft. I wanted to bury my face in it. Apparently, Dane did too because he leaned down and actually sniffed at her hair like a damn dog.

For once she didn't twitch or look nervous. Instead she smiled confidently at Dane before sitting down at the table. Dane brought her some milk and sugar and slid into the seat next to her.

"Thank you, Dane."

"You're welcome, baby."

We watched silently as she added the milk and sugar to her coffee and stirred it. My initial shock over seeing her with her hair down had faded and now my stomach was churning. Naomi didn't want us anymore.

"Why have you changed your mind about fucking us?" Dane asked abruptly.

I groaned and took a drink of my own coffee. Dane was always blunt and to the point. Normally I liked that about my best friend, but right now I wished he would shut the hell up.

"I haven't," Naomi said.

"Sweetheart, you just said that wasn't what you wanted," I said. "We both heard you."

She sipped at her coffee before setting it down on the table and staring at the steam rising from it. "No, I said I didn't want just Dane, um, fucking me. I want both of you there for my first time."

Relief flooded across Dane's face and he stroked her long hair. "Whatever you want, baby."

"No," I said, "not whatever she wants." Dane glared at me, but I continued anyway. "She needs to know, Dane."

"That you're both dominant," Naomi said. "I already know that."

"Do you even know what that means?" I asked.

"I think so," Naomi said.

She took another sip of coffee before suddenly standing and plopping herself down onto Dane's lap. Dane's face suggested he had died and gone to heaven and I swallowed my thin thread of jealousy. He buried his face in Naomi's neck and pressed a warm kiss against her skin as she put one arm around his shoulders and stared at me.

"What does it mean?" I challenged.

"It means – oh!" Her back arched. Dane was cupping her breast through her t-shirt as he licked the column of her throat.

"Dane, enough!" I said.

"Not enough," Naomi said with a little giggle.

Dane laughed and pinched her nipple through her shirt before kissing her neck. "You smell good, baby."

"Thank you." She tugged his hand away from her breast. "You'd better behave before Mason spanks you."

She giggled again as Dane squeezed her thigh. "I can't wait to see your pretty ass covered in my handprints."

"Dane!" I wanted to throw my coffee mug at him. I had no idea what the hell was happening. Naomi didn't just look different in her jeans and t-shirt with her dark hair flowing down her back, she was acting like a completely different person. What the fuck was going on?

"Why aren't you afraid of Dane anymore?" I said.

"Fuck off, Mason," Dane said with a remarkable lack of ire. He was still staring at Naomi like a lovesick puppy.

Naomi took a deep breath. "I don't know. I woke up this morning and I felt different. Now that I'm away from my father, I thought what I wanted most was to be normal. It's why I went to the party last night and tried alcohol. Only, I hated it. Not just the alcohol, but everything. There were too many people and the guys that talked to us were annoying and immature. I hated it. All I wanted was to be here with the both of you. I know that having sex with two men isn't what normal women do, and I know it makes me a whore, but I don't care. I want to have sex with both of you. You make me feel good and safe and – and happy."

Dane cupped her face and pressed a kiss against her mouth. "Having sex with both of us doesn't make you a whore, Naomi."

"Doesn't it?" she asked with honest curiosity.

"No," Dane said. "There are people who don't understand this lifestyle. They don't believe that someone can want to be with more than one person, but that's okay. We don't need them to understand it. Do we?"

"I guess not," Naomi said. "But it's not normal."

"Maybe not." Dane shrugged. "But who gets to decide what normal actually is?"

She studied him for a moment before dipping her head and kissing him. "I'm sorry I was afraid of you."

"I'll never hurt you, baby."

"I know." She smiled at both of us. "Do we have time to have sex before you go to work, do you think?"

"Fuck work," Dane said. "We're taking the day off."

Naomi grinned at him. "Really? Are you sure you can do that? I know you're busy."

"I'm the boss," Dane said. "I can do whatever I want."

He nuzzled her neck again, and I finally shook out of my goddamn stupor. "What is happening?"

"I want to have sex with both of you. I know you're both dominants and I'm okay with that," Naomi said.

"You don't know that that means," I said.

"I do, mostly," she said. "It means that you like to be in control. That you'll tell me what to do and if I don't do it, I'll be punished with a spanking."

I rubbed at the pulsing vein in the middle of my forehead. "Sweetheart, it's more than that."

"Is it though?" Dane said with a little grin.

"You know it is!" I said.

"Then tell me," Naomi said.

My frustration and my anxiety that Naomi would leave us if she really knew what we wanted in bed boiled over and the words came rushing out of me. "It means that we're going to make you wear leather cuffs and a leather collar around your neck, maybe even a leash sometimes. We're going to tie you to the bed, blindfold you, put clamps on your nipples and then tease and torment you until you're begging us to let you cum. We're going to fuck your pussy, your mouth and your ass. We'll make you call us both "sir" and do exactly what we tell you to do. If you don't, we'll punish you with spankings and floggings and we'll deny you orgasms until you're a good girl."

Dane glared at me. Naomi was giving me a thoughtful look and my mouth dropped open when she said, "But only in the bedroom, right?"

"What?" I said.

"I only have to do what you tell me in the bedroom," she said. "Outside of the bedroom, I do whatever I want."

"Of course," Dane said as I continued to stare at her with my mouth hanging open.

"Then I'm good," Naomi said. "I want to try all of those things."

Dane kissed her hard on the mouth. "Are you sure, baby?"

"I'm positive," Naomi said. "I heard what you said about being naturally submissive and I think you're right."

"Because your father is an asshole," I said hoarsely as I leaned forward. "Naomi, sweetheart, you're submissive because of an overbearing father not because you -"

"You're wrong," Naomi said. "I don't like being told what to do or how to act. I only did what my father said because I was afraid of him. I'm not afraid of you," she glanced at Dane, "I'm not afraid of either of you. But I do like it when you tell me what to do during sex. I like when Dane pinches my nipples and when you say you're going to spank me. I like it, Mason. A lot. Maybe I won't like all of it, but I'll tell you if I don't like something."

Dane kissed her again. "You'll have a safe word, baby, and we'll talk about what hard and soft limits are. Okay?"

"Okay," she said. She sat up a little straighter. "Anyway, I'm a grown woman and I can do what I want. If I want to – to get kinky with two men, then I will. You don't get to tell me I can't, Mason."

I couldn't stop the smile from crossing my face at her stubborn little scowl. "Sweetheart, I wouldn't dream of telling you what to do outside of the bedroom."

"Good," she said. "So, can we have sex now?"

Naomi smiled sweetly and I was lost. "Yes," I said. "God, yes."

Chapter Eight

Naomi

I wasn't nervous. I suppose I should have been, but I really wasn't. I was trembling and my legs felt a bit rubbery as I followed Dane up the stairs, but it wasn't from nerves. I was about to have sex for the first time, and I couldn't fucking wait.

I felt a twinge of guilt at cursing but ignored it. I could do what I wanted. Dane opened a door and Mason and I followed him into the room. It was a large bedroom with crisp white walls, red and grey accents and two big windows that filled the room with bright light. A king-size bed covered in a dark grey quilt was the centerpiece of the room. I stared at the heavy metal eye hooks screwed into the wooden headboard with an utter lack of surprise. There were matching eye hooks in the footboard, and I tapped Dane on the shoulder.

"Whose room is this?"

"Mine," he said as he stripped off his shirt. Behind me, Mason was doing the same, but my focus was on the smattering of dark hair on Dane's chest and the hard ridges of muscle that lined his abdomen. I reached out and traced the hard line of muscles, smiling a little when they jerked beneath my touch.

Dane made a hoarse noise of need as he reached for the buckle of his belt. "Mason, undress her."

Mason moved closer behind me and I automatically lifted my arms when his hands gripped the hem of my shirt. He pulled it over my head and dropped it to the floor before quickly stripping me of the rest of my clothing. My jeans were tight, and they dragged my underwear with them. Dane groaned again when my pussy was revealed. He was already naked, and he gripped his hard cock and stroked it as Mason removed his clothes.

I stood completely naked between them, soaking in the attention as Mason moved around to join Dane and they both studied me in the light. I didn't feel self-conscious at all. Instead I felt beautiful and powerful as both men looked me up and down.

When they didn't move, I said, "Is this where you bring out the collar and cuffs?"

Dane and Mason glanced at each other and a silent communication rippled between them.

"No, sweetheart," Mason said. "This time it's strictly vanilla."

"But I'm fine with it not being vanilla," I said.

"We know, baby," Dane said, "but I want your first time to be sweet."

I stared up at him as he reached out and pulled

me into his embrace. His cock brushed against my stomach, and he stroked my hair before placing a tender kiss on my mouth. "Trust me, Naomi. Okay?"

Why had I ever been afraid of him?

"Okay," I said.

Mason was pulling back the quilt and the sheet and I gripped Dane's hand as he led me to the bed. "Get in the middle, sweetheart."

I climbed into the middle of the bed and relaxed on my back as Dane and Mason stretched out on either side of me. Dane propped his head in his hand and traced my bottom lip with his thumb. "Nervous, baby?"

"No," I said. "Horny."

Mason laughed and Dane nuzzled my neck before cupping my breast. "Guess we should do something about that."

"Yes," I said breathlessly as Mason's blond head dipped toward my other breast. "Yes, I really think…oh my gosh!"

Mason's mouth had closed around my nipple. He sucked and it sent pleasure arrowing straight to my crotch. I tried not to hump the air as Dane bent his dark head and latched on to my other nipple. I clutched at both their heads, my back arching and small moaning cries escaping from my lips. I watched them both suck and tease my nipples and wetness flooded my pussy. I wiggled and moaned and pleaded as they took their time. Finally, I pulled both of their hair and Mason lifted his head.

"Patience, sweetheart."

"No," I panted. "No, I can't wait."

"Sure, you can." He traced lazy circles around my nipple with his finger and I shook my head.

"I really can't."

"Fuck," Dane muttered against my breast before giving the soft underside a quick nip. "I don't think I can wait either."

Mason laughed. "Both of you need to relax and enjoy the -"

"No!" This time I could hear the desperation in my voice and both men stared up at me. "No, not this time. I need it! I need it so much!"

I had no idea what was wrong with me other than the fact that I was twenty-three years old and was just now discovering my damn sexuality. What I knew was that I didn't want to be teased or tormented. My pussy was already clenching and unclenching uselessly, and the ache was almost more than I could stand.

I gave up on trying to convince Mason and cupped Dane's face. "Please, Dane."

"All right, baby."

"Dane -"

"No," Dane cut off Mason's protest. "We have plenty of time to tease her later, Mason. Besides, if I don't fuck her soon, I'm going to blow my load all over her goddamn thigh. Spread your legs, baby."

My legs were already spread apart but I shifted until they were splayed wide. Both Mason and Dane hooked a leg over each of mine and I moaned at the feel of their hair-roughened skin.

"Oh God," I whispered when Dane traced a circle around my belly button before trailing his fingers down to my pussy. He rubbed my clit and I would have arched off the bed if Mason and Dane hadn't been pinning me down.

"She's so fucking wet," Dane said hoarsely.

Mason was sucking on my nipple again and without lifting his head, he pressed his hand between my legs. His finger probed at my entrance and slid in as Dane rubbed again at my clit. My pussy clenched around Mason's finger and he groaned against my breast.

"Make her cum, Dane."

Dane smiled down at me and angled his mouth over mine. His tongue darted in, licking and tasting at mine, demanding my surrender as his fingers rubbed hard circles against my clit. I was already feeling that now-familiar rush of pleasure building in my lower belly and pelvis. I rocked my pussy frantically against both their hands.

Dane circled his thumb around my clit, pressed lightly on it and then circled again as Mason thrust with his finger. I was gasping and moaning into Dane's mouth and I stared up at him when he released my mouth and said, "You're so beautiful."

"Dane, please!" I moaned.

His lips lifted in a smile and he said, "You want to cum, baby? You want to cum all over our fingers?"

"Yes!" I cried out. "Yes!"

He lowered his mouth to my ear and pulled on my clit. "Then cum."

I screamed as my climax made me arch so wildly that not even Dane and Mason's weight could keep me on the bed. Vaguely through the pleasure that was soaking through my body, I heard

Mason's low groan. I was clenching around his finger with hard rhythmic pulses as Dane gently rubbed my oversensitive clit.

I tried to move away, and Dane shook his head. "No, don't move."

"Too much," I gasped. "Dane, please, too much."

Mason pulled his finger free of my pussy and I immediately tried to close my legs, tried to pull away from Dane's finger. He made a low growl of disapproval and both their legs clamped down on mine, keeping me wide open. That didn't stop me from trying to buck away but Dane's hand giving my pussy a sharp slap did. The pain and – oh God, was that pleasure mixed in too? – made me still and I stared wide-eyed at him.

"What did I tell you?" Dane said in a deep voice that made my pussy pulse with sudden need.

"Not to move," I whispered.

He gave my pussy another slap as Mason pinched my nipple hard. I cried out as pain tingled in my nipple and my pussy.

"Try again," Dane said.

I hesitated. I didn't know what he wanted from me at first but as he rubbed my sensitive clit and Mason teased my nipple with his teeth, the answer hit me.

"Not to move, sir," I said.

"Good girl," Dane said. I flushed from his approval and he sucked on my bottom lip before moving his hand to my stomach. He rested it against my skin as Mason released my nipple.

"Your pussy is ours," Dane said. My muscles

fluttered under his hand and he rubbed my stomach. "Do you understand, baby? If we want to touch it, we will. If we want to fuck it, we will. Telling us to stop touching you will only get you a spanking. Is that clear?"

"Yes, sir," I said.

I wanted to point out to them that this didn't seem like vanilla sex, but I was afraid they would switch back to the vanilla if I did. I liked what they were doing and saying to me – wrong or right – and I didn't want them to stop.

"Maybe we should get the collar for her," Dane said. A new thrill went through me, but Mason shook his head.

"No, not this time."

Dane was obviously going to argue but Mason arched one blond eyebrow at him. "Next time."

"Fine."

Dane looked so much like a little boy who had been denied his toy that I couldn't help but giggle. He grinned at me and rolled away to sit up on the bed as Mason pressed a kiss on my shoulder. "Are you ready, sweetheart?"

"Yes," I said.

Dane was rolling on a condom and I touched Mason's face hesitantly. "Will you stay while we're…"

Mason nodded. "If you want me to."

"I do." I reached down and wrapped my fingers around his stiff cock. "Maybe I could touch you while Dane is, um, in me." I flushed a little. I was twenty-three years old and still had a hard time saying the word 'fucking'.

Mason groaned before pulling my hand away. "No, sweetheart. I want you to concentrate solely on the experience."

"But -"

"No buts," he said as Dane rolled over to face us.

I stared at his cock. It seemed even larger than the last time I saw it and for the first time, a trickle of anxiety went through me. As if sensing it, both Dane and Mason petted me like I was a nervous cat before Dane kissed me.

"I'll go slow, baby. I promise."

"I know," I said.

"Spread your legs for me."

I spread my legs wide, smiling at Mason when he cupped my thigh and squeezed it reassuringly as Dane knelt between my legs. He rubbed his cock against my clit, and I moaned. He moved lower, probing at my wet entrance and I smiled encouragingly.

"Please, Dane."

He pressed forward. A vein was throbbing in his forehead and the look on his face suggested he was using every ounce of his willpower to not just ram into me.

"Okay, sweetheart?" Mason's voice murmured close to my ear. I turned my head and smiled at him as Dane pushed harder.

"Yes, it's good. It's – ouch!" I immediately blushed and stared at Dane with embarrassment. "I'm sorry."

"Mason," Dane gritted out between clenched teeth, "distract her."

Mason scooted closer until his hard body was pressed against my side. I could feel his cock rubbing against my thigh as he kissed me slowly and thoroughly. He coaxed my tongue into his mouth and sucked on it as his hand cupped my breast and teased the nipple.

When he finally released my mouth, I was panting and making little hip jerks against Dane. "Oh please," I moaned. I had forgotten about the pain. When Mason moved back and Dane propped himself up with his hands on either side of my head, I clung to his narrow waist.

"Please, Dane."

He pushed forward with one hard thrust. There was pain, more than I expected, and I closed my eyes against the sting of it as Dane stayed perfectly still above me. Mason crooned softly in my ear and his warm hand stroked my side and hip as Dane leaned down and kissed me.

"I'm sorry, baby," he whispered against my lips.

"It's okay," I said. "I just need a minute."

"Take all the time you need, sweetheart," Mason said. Dane made a low groan and I couldn't help the smile that crossed my lips despite the lingering pain.

"I don't think Dane can wait that long," I said.

"Whatever you need," Dane muttered. The vein was throbbing in his forehead again and he was biting his bottom lip compulsively.

I moved a little beneath him as Dane groaned again. I was pinned to the bed by his cock and the heavy weight of his body, and I rubbed my thighs against his hips as pleasure trickled through me.

"Okay?" Mason said.

"Yes," I said. "I like it."

Mason grinned at Dane who withdrew a little before pushing forward. His thick cock rubbed against my inner walls and I made a soft little moan as my hands slipped around his waist and pressed into his lower back.

"Do that again," I demanded.

Dane repeated the motion as Mason encouraged me to brace my feet on the bed. I stared up at Dane in fascination as he made long, slow strokes in and out of my pussy.

"You feel so good, baby," he moaned.

He was already starting to speed up and I made a few awkward motions with my hips, trying to meet his rhythm. After only a few seconds, I found it and I squeezed his waist as I met each of his strokes. He moaned and drove in and out as a dark flush rose from his chest and up his neck. He was panting, and my eyes widened when he suddenly stiffened and drove in one final time. There was a brief flash of pain and I squeezed his hips with my thighs as Dane made a hoarse shout and his back arched. The cords in his neck stood out in stark relief and he shuddered all over when I lifted my head and licked his collarbone.

"Fuck!" He bent his head and kissed me hard on the mouth.

I returned his kiss and smiled when he pressed his forehead against mine. "I'm sorry, baby."

"For what?"

"I lost control."

"I didn't mind," I said.

He turned to Mason and said almost defensively, "She's so fucking tight. I couldn't help it."

Mason didn't reply and Dane eased out of me before lying on his back next to me. I missed the warmth and weight of his body almost immediately and I turned to Mason. He was staring at my tits and rubbing his cock with rough, hard strokes.

"Mason?"

"Yeah, sweetheart," he panted as he continued to stare at my tits.

"I want you too."

His hand slowed on his cock and his whole body jerked before he shook his head. "No, you're too sore."

"I'm not," I said. "Please, Mason."

"I shouldn't," he said in a low voice as his gaze dropped to my pussy.

"Yes," I insisted.

He hesitated a moment longer before sitting up. "Dane, condom."

Dane didn't move, just continued to stare up at the ceiling with his chest heaving.

"Dane!"

I smiled a little and rolled to my side before leaning over Dane. He groaned when he felt my breasts brush against his chest, and he cupped my ass and squeezed it as I opened the nightstand and grabbed a condom.

I eased away from him but couldn't resist pressing a quick kiss against his mouth. He cupped my head and deepened the kiss before letting me go. "You're amazing, Naomi."

"So are you," I said before lying on my back again and handing the condom to Mason.

He rolled it on and quickly moved between my legs. "Naomi, are you sure?"

"Yes," I said. "Unless you don't want to?"

"Trust me, sweetheart, you asking me to fuck you is a dream come true. I'm so worked up I'm not even sure I won't embarrass myself like Dane did."

Dane huffed out a laugh. "You have no fucking idea how tight she is."

"Mason," I tried to urge him down by grabbing his forearms and pulling on them. "Don't make me wait any longer."

"Yes, sweetheart."

He guided his cock to my pussy and pushed in. There was no pain this time, but he stared anxiously at me once he was deep inside of me. "Sweetheart?"

"It's good." I wrapped my legs around his waist, hooking my feet together in the small of his back.

He groaned and muttered a curse, and I gasped when he made two hard thrusts.

Dane barked out laughter. "Who's losing control now?"

"Oh my God," Mason moaned. "Fuck!"

Dane turned on his side and propped his head in his hand again as Mason drove in and out. Unlike Dane, he wasn't even trying to keep control and he pushed harder and faster as I tried to match his quick rhythm.

I squeaked in surprise when Dane snaked his hand between us. His fingers found my clit and rubbed.

"Oh my God!" I shouted as hot pleasure flowed through me. I was the one suddenly losing control as Mason's thick cock plunged in and out of my pussy, and Dane's rough fingers rubbed my swollen and sensitive clit.

I bucked erratically against Mason and when Dane pinched my clit, I screamed and climaxed in a dizzying rush of white-hot pleasure and blinding light. I had no idea if Mason was cumming or not as I shuddered and moaned beneath him.

Dane's warm breath brushed my ear as he kissed the sensitive spot just below my lobe. I made a soft grunt of pain when heavy weight landed on me.

"Mason, get off of her," Dane said before giving him a shove.

Mason pulled out of me and collapsed beside me. His eyes were closed and sweat dotted his forehead. I touched his chest tentatively. "Mason? Did you cum?"

"Like a fucking fire hydrant," he said.

Dane snorted before pulling off his condom and dropping it into the trash can next to the bed. Mason rolled off the bed, staggering a little on his feet. He peeled off the condom and walked naked to the bathroom.

Dane brushed my hair back from my face before threading his fingers through it. "You okay, baby?"

"Yes," I said. "It was wonderful. Thank you."

"I'm the one who needs to thank you."

My eyelids were drifting shut and despite it being mid-morning, I was pleasantly sleepy.

"You're welcome."

His low laugh made me smile. His big hand rested on my stomach and he caressed my skin. "You look tired, baby. You need a nap."

"Hmm," I said.

He didn't reply and I dragged my eyelids open. Shit, I was being really presumptuous. I started to sit up, falling flat on my back when Dane's hand pressed down against my midsection. "Where are you going?"

"I can nap in my own bed," I said before a yawn nearly split my head in two. "I don't want to assume that I can sleep in your bed."

He scowled. Last week that scowl would have sent anxiety racing through my veins, now it only made me think how cute he looked when he was getting worked up over something.

"You're allowed to sleep in my bed," he said. "Mine or Mason's. Whenever you want, Naomi."

"Hmm, that's so nice of you," I said as my eyelids closed again.

I turned on my side, burying my face into the pillow as Dane pulled the covers over both of us. "Go to sleep, baby."

"Sure, okay," I mumbled before sleep overtook me.

Chapter Nine

Mason

"Did you enjoy your bath, sweetheart?" I sat down on the couch next to Naomi. Dane was cleaning up the lunch dishes in the kitchen, and Naomi smiled a little when his off-key singing drifted into the living room.

"Yes, thank you. And thank you for lunch, it was delicious. I could have helped clean up," she said.

I shrugged. "Dane and I have a pretty good rhythm. I cook, he cleans."

She was staring at me like I'd grown a second head.

"What?"

She looked away, a slight blush in her cheeks. "It's weird to me to see guys doing, um, household chores. In my family, it's the woman's responsibility."

"Well, we do have a cleaning service that comes in weekly but when we were young and broke, we did our own housecleaning."

"Have you and Dane always lived together?"

I nodded. "Yeah. We met in high school, were roommates in university, and moved in together after."

"When, um…"

She licked her lips, her fingers twining restlessly around each other in her lap.

"When did we start sleeping with women together?" Her sweet face was so easy to read.

She nodded and I put my arm along the back of the couch, secretly satisfied when she scooted a little closer and relaxed against me.

"We've been doing the threesome thing since university," I said.

"Do you ever sleep with women separately?"

"We used to." I touched Naomi's hair, amazed all over again by how soft it was. "But rarely now. I don't remember the last time I slept with a woman without Dane there."

"Three years ago." Dane joined us in the living room and sat down on the other side of Naomi. "You hooked up with her on your vacation in Hawaii."

"What about you?" Naomi said to Dane.

"It's been years," Dane admitted. "I prefer to have Mason joining us."

"It's my preference as well," I said.

"Have you guys ever, uh, hooked up with each other?" Naomi asked. Her face was bright red and I could almost smell her embarrassment.

"Nah," Dane said. "We're only into the ladies."

"What happens when one of you wants to get

married and have a family?" Naomi asked.

Dane glanced at me. We'd talked about that very thing numerous times in the past. It had always been our hope that we'd find one woman who would be willing to share us. We knew it was a long shot, but the idea of living separate lives didn't appeal to either of us.

I was trying to think of a way to word it when Dane's usual bluntness kicked in.

"We want one woman to share us both. We know it isn't traditional but that's what we want."

"Oh," Naomi said.

I was surprised Dane hadn't told Naomi he wanted her to share us both. My best friend was head over heels in love with her and while I understood it, hell, I was halfway to being in love with her myself, I was thankful he hadn't said it. Naomi wouldn't want to be with us forever. How could she? She hardly knew us. Lust didn't equate to love.

She was a decade younger than us and she'd barely lived her life. She deserved to go out and meet new people, explore everything the world had to offer, rather than settle down into a life of being a wife to two men. A mother to our children.

My chest tightened. I wanted kids and so did Dane. A whole houseful of them.

"Do you want to get married?" Dane asked.

"Um, eventually." Naomi fidgeted against me. "You know, when I find the right person. My original plan was to put aside enough money to get my own place so I could escape my father. After that, I was going to save up some more money and look at taking night classes. A few of the colleges have programs where you can take evening courses to get your degree."

"What were you thinking of taking?" I asked.

"Interior design." Naomi fidgeted again. "I like decorating and designing rooms and I... I think I would be good at it. Or at least, I enjoy it enough to try and make a living from it. But now I'm revising my plan."

"Why's that?" I said.

She stared at her restless fingers. "Well, I know you said it wasn't necessary, but I want to pay back the money you gave my father. Would you be open to talking about a payment schedule? I was thinking maybe -"

"No," Dane said.

Thunderclouds danced across his forehead and I could practically see the steam rolling out from his ears.

"Dane, chill out," I said.

"You're not paying us back," Dane said. "Ever."

She frowned at him. "Why do you get to take away my choice in this?"

"Because your choice is ridiculous," Dane said.

"Dane!" I glared at him, but Naomi was starting to giggle.

"You're ridiculous," she said but her tone was soft, and her look was affectionate.

"We don't need the money," Dane said. "We've got loads of it, more than we'll ever spend in our lifetimes."

"Oh my God," I said. "You sound like a

pretentious douchebag, Dane."

Naomi laughed. "Seriously though, are you guys millionaires?"

"We've invested well," I said.

"Yup," Dane said.

Naomi laughed again. God, I loved the sound of it. "That's very cool."

I kissed her temple, inhaling the strawberry scent of her hair. "We've worked our asses off the last few years to get to this point and neither of us could think of a better use of the money than helping you."

"Helping my father you mean." Her voice was tinged with bitterness. "I really am sorry that you had to buy me like some prized cow from my own father."

"We didn't," I said. "We helped out a friend, someone we care about very much. That's all."

She stared up at me, her beautiful blue eyes dark with emotion. "You guys saved my life, you know. And I won't ever forget it."

Dane's big hand wrapped around hers and squeezed. "We were happy to help, baby. Anything you need, you just ask us."

"I think I'm good for now," she said.

"Oh yeah? Because I saw your cell phone in the garbage," I said.

"My father paid for the plan. He'll probably have it cancelled by this time tomorrow," she said. "Besides, I don't want to keep anything that he gave me."

"Why don't we go out and get you a new one right now?" I stood and pulled Naomi to her feet.

"What? No," she said. "I didn't mean – that is, I'm not asking you to get me a new cell phone. I can get my own phone and plan. Plus, we need to talk about what rent and grocery costs will be."

"You're not paying rent. Food bill is split three ways," I said.

"I have to pay rent," she said, "I can't just -"

"Do you have any credit history?" Dane steamrolled right over her protests. "A credit card in your name?"

"No," she said. I could practically see her deflating in front of us.

"It's hard to get a phone plan without some kind of credit score," Dane said.

"I'll just buy a cheap phone and get, like, a pay as you go plan," she said.

"Or, you could let us buy you a better phone and add you to one of our plans while you apply for a credit card and build up your credit rating," I said.

She chewed at her bottom lip. I wanted to lean down and suck that bottom lip into my mouth. I wanted to take her back upstairs to the bedroom and sink myself into her exquisite pussy again.

Instead, I said, "It's the best plan, Naomi."

"It's the plan where I owe you more money," she said.

"It's a gift," Dane said. "A thank you for giving us the best sex of our lives gift."

She turned a fiery shade of red. "I know that isn't true. Someone with zero experience is not going to give you the best sex of your life."

Dane pulled her into his embrace, his hands reaching down to squeeze handfuls of that perfect ass. "Baby, your pussy was so tight and wet and perfect that when I came, I'm pretty sure my soul left my body for a few minutes."

"Jesus, you're such a fucking cheeseball," I said. "But the cheeseball is right, Naomi. Your pussy is outstanding."

"Outstanding?" Naomi burst into laughter before kissing Dane and then me. "You guys are great for a girl's ego."

"Does that mean you'll let us buy you a phone and set you up on a plan?"

She nodded. "Yes. Thank you so much. I know I keep saying this, but I really am so thankful that you're helping me."

"It's our pleasure." I pressed a soft kiss against her lips.

ஐ ஒ

Mason

"Look at this!" Naomi plopped down on the couch and showed me the screen of her new phone. "It has built-in ring tones. I can choose one for you and one for Dane, so I'll know who's calling or texting without even looking at the screen. How cool is that?"

Her delight over the smallest things was something I loved about her. While we were out getting her a phone, Dane had managed to talk her into letting us buy her a laptop and a tablet as well, quieting her protests by pointing out she would need both for college.

"I'm glad you like your new phone,

sweetheart," I said.

She beamed at me, the happiness shining out of her in pure sweet waves. "I love it so much. I've never had such nice things in my life. You guys totally spoiled me today."

"You deserve to be spoiled," I said.

She laughed. "I don't, but thank you for saying that. Dinner was also amazing. We didn't really eat out a lot in my family so that was definitely a treat. Thank you."

"You're welcome," I said.

She studied her phone again before glancing at the doorway. "Where did Dane go?"

I didn't reply right away. During dinner when Naomi had excused herself to use the restroom, Dane and I had talked about tonight. I was anxious to see how Naomi would respond to sex that wasn't strictly vanilla. Dane didn't want to push her too far, too fast, but I argued that it was better for us to find out now if she really did like kink and if she enjoyed being dominated in bed, before we became too involved with her.

Dane still wanted to wait, still insisted that he would be happy with just vanilla sex, but I knew him better than that. Hell, even this morning hadn't been completely vanilla. Neither of us could help it. We wanted to dominate Naomi in the bedroom and denying what we wanted would only result in frustration for all three of us.

"Mason?" Naomi's soft hand rested on my thigh and my cock immediately went to half-mast. Fuck, she had no idea what her simple touch did to me.

"He's waiting for us in the bedroom, sweetheart."

Her cheeks flushed. "Why didn't you say something earlier?"

"Because you were excited about your new phone."

She chucked the phone on the couch beside her. "Screw the new phone."

I bellowed laughter and her timid smile turned more natural. "I didn't actually mean that because I love the phone, but I also really want to have sex with you guys again."

I stood and she took my offered hand, following me out of the living room and up the stairs. My stomach was tense with nerves. What if she didn't like what she saw when I opened the door. What if her assurances that she was willing to try kink in the bedroom was just something she had said to make us happy?

As much as I wanted a cuffed and collared Naomi on her knees in front of me, I wouldn't – *couldn't* – do that to her if it wasn't something she really wanted.

We stepped into the bedroom. Dane was standing beside the bed, his normally inscrutable expression replaced with an anxiety I'd never seen on him before. Unease trickled into my belly. If Naomi wasn't into the kink or being dominated, did Dane love her so much that he would deny who he really was? What he really wanted?

"Dane, what's…"

Naomi's soft voice trailed off as her cheeks pinked. I followed her gaze to the bed, wondering what she thought of the pink leather collar and matching cuffs sitting in front of the pillow. Wondering what she thought of the delicate but strong silver chains that were pooled on the bed in front of the cuffs.

"Baby, are you all right?" Dane couldn't hide his anxiety.

"I guess it's not just vanilla sex tonight, huh?" Naomi said.

"You don't have to do anything you don't want to," Dane assured her.

She turned toward me, and I smiled at her. "You don't have to wear them, Naomi."

"I want to."

That simple statement sent my cock from half-mast straight into a throbbing painful erection.

"C'mere, baby." Dane's voice had turned eager.

She took a deep breath and dropped my hand, walking to Dane who had picked up the collar. She touched the soft leather before taking another deep breath. "How, um, how many other women have worn this?"

"No one." I'd moved up behind them and she twitched when I pressed a soft kiss against the back of her shoulder. "It and the cuffs are brand new."

"When did you buy them?" she asked Dane. "I just agreed this morning to try some, uh, kinky stuff and we've been together all day."

She studied him before turning to me. "Is he blushing?"

I laughed. "He's blushing."

Dane made a grunt of annoyance. "I don't blush."

"Why is he blushing?" Naomi asked with a small smile.

"Because he doesn't want to admit that he bought the collar and cuffs for you about a week after you started working for him."

Her mouth dropped open. Mother of God, the idea of pushing her to her knees and filling that beautiful mouth with my cock was almost too difficult to resist.

"You bought it… but, why?" she said.

"Because I wanted to fuck you the very second I saw you," Dane said.

"You have such a way with words," I said.

Naomi was blushing and smiling. "I like how blunt he is. Until the two of you, I didn't really think I was that pretty, my mom always said I was too fat to find a good-looking boy, so it's nice to know you want me even if I am fat. It… it makes me feel good."

Without even thinking about it, I put my arm around Naomi's waist and gave her two hard slaps to the ass. She squealed and rubbed at her butt through her jeans as Dane gave me a *what the fuck* look.

"If you say unkind things about yourself, you get a spanking. Is that clear?" I said.

"Yes," she said.

I spanked her again, my cock pressing against my jeans at the sound it made when my hand connected with her ass. Fuck, I wished she was naked, wished I could see the bright red of my handprint fill in on her pale ass.

"Ouch!" She rubbed her ass again, glaring at

me. "I didn't say anything bad about myself."

"No, but you didn't address me properly. Try again," I said.

"Yes, sir," she said, but there was impudence in her voice.

My hand itched. I couldn't wait to spank that impudence out of her. Couldn't wait to hear her moaning and begging for more. Couldn't wait to see how wet her little pussy would be after her spanking.

Slow down, asshole.

I pushed my hands behind my back as Naomi stared up at Dane before lifting up her long hair. Dane's hands were shaking as he placed the collar around her neck and buckled it. It was snug but not too tight and he handed me a cuff. Naomi held out her wrists obediently as we put a cuff around each wrist. She hadn't said a word, but her eyes were bright, and her cheeks were flushed, and I knew her well enough now to know she was turned on.

My cock was impossibly hard, and Dane had already stripped off his t-shirt and was unbuttoning his jeans.

"How do they look?" Naomi said.

"Beautiful." Dane shoved his jeans down his legs, and I heard the audible click in Naomi's throat when she stared at his dick.

"Come here, baby." Dane held out his hand to Naomi.

As he stripped her naked, I attached the chains to the eye hooks embedded in the headboard before removing my own clothes. By the time I joined them, Dane had Naomi completely naked and his hand was between her legs.

She moaned and wiggled, her hands clutching at his broad shoulders as I stared at her perfect ass. I was going to fuck that perfect ass in the very near future and just the thought made precum drip from my dick.

Dane grinned at me before kissing Naomi on the mouth. "Baby, Mason needs your help."

She whined when he removed his hand from between her legs. His fingers were dripping wet and more precum leaked out of my slit. Fuck, I needed her mouth so bad.

Dane turned Naomi to face me. Her face was flushed and her eyes bright with need. She stared at my cock as Dane cupped her tits and tugged on her nipples. "You're going to be our good girl and suck Mason's cock."

"I've never, um…."

"We know." Dane kissed the side of her neck just above her collar.

He pressed on her shoulders and I stepped forward as Naomi knelt, her knees sinking into the plush carpet. Dane stroked her long hair as she stared up at him.

"Do you want a pillow to kneel on, sweetheart?" I said.

"No, I'm good. Just a little nervous," she said.

"Don't be nervous, baby," Dane petted her hair again, "nothing you do will be wrong. I promise."

"Except for biting," I said solemnly. "No biting."

Naomi stared wide-eyed at me and when I winked and snapped my teeth at her, she burst into sweet giggles. "No biting… got it."

I stepped closer until my cock was almost touching her full mouth. Ignoring my urge to just shove my dick down her throat, I gripped the base as Dane stroked Naomi's hair. "Have a taste of Mason's cock, baby."

I groaned when her soft pink tongue licked her lips. I couldn't wait to have that tongue on my… motherfucking hell!

I groaned, my hips jerking forward when Naomi's tongue licked away the precum beading out of my slit. She made a startled cry, leaning back against Dane's thighs as she stared up at me. "I – was that wrong?"

"No," I rasped, tightening my hand around the base of my dick to stop myself from cumming. Jesus, what the hell was wrong with me?

"Control, Mason," Dane said.

"I know," I said. Heat was rising in my cheeks. Since when the fuck did I almost cum from having a woman lick my dick?

Not just a woman. Naomi. The girl you love.

I took a deep breath, pushing down my inner voice. I liked Naomi a lot, but I hadn't known her long enough to be in love. I wasn't a fucking romantic sap like Dane.

"Try again, baby," Dane encouraged.

Naomi took a deep breath as I willed myself to find the control Dane was talking about. This time, Naomi closed her mouth around the head of my cock and my head fell back, my hand fisting the shaft as Naomi sucked tentatively.

She released me with a soft pop and stared up at

Dane. "I like the way he tastes."

"That's good, baby," Dane said.

"I want to taste you," she said.

A strangled sound of need escaped Dane's throat and then he was standing next to me, his hand fisting his own cock. "Go ahead."

Naomi smiled and sucked on the head of Dane's cock. I coughed out a laugh when he immediately pumped his hips, sliding more of his dick into her mouth.

"Control," I croaked.

Dane flipped me the bird before stroking Naomi's cheek with his fingertips. "Good, baby. Clean me off with your tongue."

She did what he asked, licking the head of his dick until the precum was gone before turning toward me. She cleaned me off as well, the soft slide of her tongue made my eyes roll back in my head.

"Good," Dane said. "Take more of his cock."

"No," I muttered. "Probably not a good... oh fuck!"

My hands shot out and gripped the back of Naomi's skull when she slid more of her mouth down my dick. I fucked her face with three hard thrusts, pulling back when I brushed the back of her throat and she made a strangled sound of surprise.

"Sorry," I panted. "Sweetheart, I'm sorry. You okay?"

"Yes." She touched her red and swollen lips before suddenly grinning. "I like this. A lot."

With renewed vigor she attacked my cock, sucking hard as one small hand wrapped around my shaft. She sucked with enthusiasm. Her method was a bit sloppy and it was obvious that she wasn't completely certain what to do, but I didn't fucking care. Naomi had never looked more beautiful to me and her warm, wet mouth felt almost as good as her pussy.

I let her suck me for a few more minutes before pulling away. My balls were tightening and if I let her continue, I'd cum and never hear the end of it from Dane.

When Naomi tried to suck on my cock again, I wrapped my hand in her hair and gave it a sharp tug. She pouted up at me. "I want to suck on your cock, Mason."

Dane leaned down and slapped her hard on her bare ass. She squealed, her body jerked, and I loosened my grip on her hair so it didn't pull too tightly.

"Ow! Dane!"

He spanked her again. "What do you call us in the bedroom, Naomi?"

"Sir," she said. "I'm sorry, sir."

I released her hair and Dane's hand took my place. He tugged hard, guiding Naomi's mouth to his dick. "Open."

She opened her mouth and I watched as Dane slid his cock deep into her mouth.

"Dane, easy."

He ignored me, tightening his grip on Naomi's hair when she tried to lean back. "No, baby. Relax. Breathe through your nose. Good girl. Suck hard and lick the shaft. Good."

I fisted my cock, rubbing slowly as I watched

Dane teach Naomi how to suck cock. I was impressed with his self-control. I was barely hanging on just watching Naomi's lips slide up and down Dane's cock.

I rubbed a little harder, watching as, with Dane's urging, Naomi first licked and then sucked on Dane's balls before returning to his dick and sucking obediently. Fuck, she was so beautiful. The collar around her neck fit perfectly and I was suddenly itching to bury my face in her pussy.

"Dane," I said. "put her on the bed."

He pulled out of Naomi's mouth, shaking his head when she pouted up at him. "That's it for now, baby. On your feet."

He helped her to her feet and kissed her hard on the mouth before guiding her toward the bed. She stretched out on her bed, giving Dane a hesitant look when he picked up the small silver chains. "Hands above your head."

"Dane, slow down. We need a safe word." I sat on the bed next to Naomi and rested my hand on the gentle curve of her belly. "Give us a safe word, honey."

"I don't... I mean, I'm not sure what I should choose," she said.

"How about red?" I said. "It's easy and simple."

"Okay."

I could feel her muscles quivering under my touch, and I stroked her smooth skin. "If at any time you want us to stop or you don't like something we're doing, just say 'red' and we'll stop immediately."

She glanced at Dane who said, "We won't be angry if you say it. I promise."

"I know," she said. "I trust you both."

She lifted her hands above her head and Dane leaned down to kiss her again. "Thank you, baby. This means an incredible amount to both of us. Remember, all you have to do is say red and everything stops."

"If you're feeling unsure, you can also say yellow," I said, my hand moving up to caress her tits. "We'll stop and check in with you to see if you want to keep going."

She giggled nervously. "It suddenly feels so... I don't know – formal, almost."

Dane smiled but his tone was serious. "Rules and safe words are very important, Naomi. We still need to talk about hard and soft limits but I'm confident that everything we do to you right now will be something you want. So, we can talk about limits in the next day or two. Okay?"

"Okay," she said. "What exactly are you going to do to me right now?"

Dane's grin widened as he connected the silver chains to the metal loops in the cuffs around Naomi's wrists. Naomi tugged lightly and then a bit harder. Her face flushed when she realized she was truly trapped.

"What's your safe word, sweetheart?" I spread her legs and stretched out on my stomach before kissing just above her pussy.

"R-red," she moaned.

Her hands clenched into fists as Dane knelt on the bed next to her upper body and pulled on her nipples. "Good. If you want us to stop, what do you say?"

"I say – oh my God!"

I had licked her pussy from her entrance all the way up her soaking wet slit. I licked again and Dane laughed when Naomi made a loud squeal and her entire body jerked on the bed. "You like that, baby?"

"Oh my God," Naomi whispered. She was trembling, and I pressed a kiss against the wet lips of her pussy as she said, "Do that again."

"This?" I kissed her pussy again.

Naomi shook her head. "No, the other thing."

"Say it," Dane said.

Her face went bright red and she closed her eyes. "I can't."

"You can." Dane's voice was hard and relentless. "Tell Mason what you want him to do."

"Please," she moaned. "Mason, please."

I nipped the lips of her pussy, and her little squeal of shock made my dick rock fucking hard. "Try again."

"Sir, please," she whimpered. "Please, um, lick my pussy."

"Good girl," I said before licking up her slit again.

She cried out, her legs moving restlessly on the bed as I parted her pussy lips and stared at her pink and swollen clit. Had I ever seen anything more beautiful?

I glanced up when Naomi moaned again. Dane had bent his head and was sucking and licking her nipples. Her back arched and I licked her clit with the tip of my tongue.

She squealed, her body jerking again, and Dane raised his head to grin at her. "What's wrong?"

"I don't... oh fuck!" Naomi shouted.

Dane laughed as I dived back into her pussy and set to work. I licked and nibbled her clit, teasing it with my tongue and lips as Naomi moaned, her curvy body writhing on the bed. When her legs clamped around my head, I pried them apart before sucking hard on her clit.

She screamed, her arms pulling against her restraints, and her upper body rising off the bed. Dane pressed hard on her sternum, pushing her back onto the bed. "How does she taste?"

"Like a sweet peach," I said before giving her clit another suck.

Naomi cried out, her thighs straining against my grip. I slid my finger into her pussy, smiling when her muscles tightened around my finger. Dane rested his arm across Naomi's midsection, holding her still as he leaned down to her pussy. "I want a taste."

I moved to my knees, keeping my finger buried deep in Naomi's tight warmth. I watched Naomi's face as Dane licked her clit, reveling in the look of hot lust and pleasure that flooded across it. She was so damn beautiful, and I couldn't believe she was ours.

"Fuck, she tastes damn good," Dane said.

"Told you." I added another finger and worked them in and out of Naomi's slick pussy as Dane licked and sucked her clit. The chains rattled against the headboard as Naomi twisted and turned against Dane's arm. The loud moans and cries of bliss falling from her lips were the sweetest aphrodisiac, and I thrust harder as Dane tugged and pulled on her clit with his mouth.

Her body tensed, her hips arched up, and she screamed her release as wetness flooded my fingers. Her muscles clamped down on my fingers and I groaned, wishing like hell it was my dick she was clamping down on. Dane was cleaning her with his tongue, and she made a harsh cry, her body shuddering wildly.

"Too much," she gasped.

I slid my fingers out of her as Dane sat up and wiped his face on the sheet before reaching into the nightstand. He tossed a condom my way and I rolled it on. Dane moved to the head of the bed and knelt next to Naomi's head. He smoothed away the hair from her face while I pushed her thighs wide and pressed the head of my cock against her opening.

"Naomi, look at me," Dane said.

Her eyelids fluttered up and she stared at him with dazed pleasure. "That felt so good, sir."

Dane pressed a kiss against her mouth. "Mason's going to fuck your pussy and I'm going to fuck your mouth. Be my good girl and swallow all of my cum. Do you understand?"

"I… yes, sir."

Naomi's voice was faint and drowsy with pleasure. I smiled a little as I stroked her smooth inner thighs. Our girl was tired, and we'd let her sleep… after she pleased us.

"Naomi," Dane's voice had turned stern. "Look

at me. Keep those beautiful eyes on my face as you suck my dick."

"Yes, sir," Naomi said in that pleasure-soaked voice.

Dane pressed his cock against Naomi's lips, tracing them with the head until they were covered in a sheen of his precum. "Open, Naomi."

Her mouth dropped open and I slid my dick into her pussy as Dane slid his into her mouth. I groaned, my fingers tightening on her thighs. Her pussy was so fucking tight. Dane was feeding her more of his cock and I pushed and retreated in a slow rhythm until Naomi's tiny pussy was stuffed full of every inch of my cock.

She made a muffled sound of protest, her thighs squeezing around my hips and her hands clenching into fists. Dane stroked her hair soothingly before cupping her breast and teasing her nipple with his fingers. "You're doing so good, baby. Just relax and let Mason fuck your beautiful pussy."

Her thighs relaxed and I rubbed them roughly before making a few shallow thrusts. She moaned, the sound muffled by Dane's thick cock.

"Jesus," Dane said, "I am not going to fucking last, Mason."

"Me neither," I said hoarsely.

"Fuck." Dane rubbed his thumb along Naomi's cheekbone, studying the way her lips stretched around his shaft. "Baby, you look so fucking hot with your mouth and pussy stuffed full of our cocks. You're gonna make both me and Mason cum so hard."

I could see the look of satisfaction in her gaze

and Dane grinned before pumping his dick in and out of her mouth. "That's my good girl. Keep looking at me. Use your tongue… good. That's right. You're so good at this, baby."

While Dane praised her, I cupped her thighs in my hands, shifted her slightly, and drove in nice and deep. Her little pussy squeezed tight around me and I muttered a curse under my breath before thrusting in and out. Dane was moving harder and faster as well, but he pulled completely out of Naomi's mouth every third or fourth stroke to give her a chance to safe word.

"Okay, baby?" he said, his voice hoarse with need.

"Yes," she moaned as my heavy balls slapped against her. "Yes, please don't stop."

He slid back into her mouth and I thrust harder before pressing my thumb against her swollen clit and rubbing in rough circles. Naomi cried out around Dane's cock and he pulled out immediately, studying her anxiously.

"Oh God," Naomi moaned. "I think – I might cum again."

Dane grinned. "Not think. You are going to cum again."

He pushed his dick past her lips before she could respond, fucking her mouth with long heavy strokes as I fucked her pussy and rubbed her clit. Her pussy was tightening and releasing me in a rhythm that was making my cum-loaded balls tighten. I was about ten seconds from cumming, and I muttered a curse and rubbed Naomi's clit harder.

"Fuck, sweetheart, you need to cum for us," I said. "Cum for us right now." I pinched her clit and Naomi went over the edge, her beautiful body shaking, her feet drumming on the bed, and her pussy clamping down on my dick like a goddamn vice.

I shouted her name and pushed in deep, my own climax pulled out of me by the milking of her pussy. As wave after wave of pleasure crested over me, I was only vaguely aware of Dane's own shout of release, of the way he gripped Naomi's head as he came deep in her mouth.

I pulled out before I collapsed on top of Naomi and moved to the side of the bed, removing the condom with shaking fingers and tossing it in the trash. I laid on my back, panting and trying to catch my breath as beside me, Dane released the chains that held Naomi captive and then lowered her arms. He rubbed them briskly before lying on his side next to her. I squinted at them both. There were traces of Dane's cum on Naomi's lips and Dane smiled approvingly when Naomi licked it away.

"Good girl," he said before kissing her.

She smiled languidly at him. "I feel so good right now. Those were the best orgasms ever. I had no idea having my pussy eaten would feel that good."

Dane grinned. "I'm glad you enjoyed it, baby. Turn on your side."

"Can't... too weak," she said.

He laughed and helped her roll onto her side before spooning her. "Are your arms okay?"

"Hmm, yeah," Naomi said before yawning. "I

think I liked being tied down and helpless while you did that."

"That's good. We liked it too." Dane kissed the back of her shoulder, his hand cupping her breast and his fingers toying lazily with her nipple.

Naomi cracked open one eyelid and squinted at me. "Mason? Did you enjoy it? You're really quiet."

"Sweetheart, it was fucking amazing," I said. "I'm quiet because I forgot how to form words for a minute there."

She giggled, and I reached out and took her hand, squeezing it tight.

"Thank you for, um, eating my pussy," Naomi said. "I enjoyed it a lot."

The seriousness of her tone made me want to smile but instead I said, "You're welcome, Naomi."

She yawned again and Dane pulled the quilt over all three of us. "Go to sleep, baby."

Chapter Ten

Naomi

"Shit." I stared at the dropped file before looking around Dane's empty office a bit guiltily. Cursing still felt forbidden and wrong and there was a part of me that half-expected my father to pop up and scold me for my foul language.

I took a deep breath. That wasn't going to happen. My father would never again get to tell me what to do and there was absolutely nothing wrong with cursing. I smiled a little, tracing the edge of Dane's desk.

Two days ago, while being fucked by Dane over the back of the couch, I'd practically screamed the word 'fuck' at the top of my lungs. Once I'd gotten over the bone-rattling orgasm, I'd apologized for my coarseness. Dane had just laughed and told me that people who cursed had a higher intelligence level than those who didn't.

I continued to trace the top of Dane's desk. He was out at a meeting and I wasn't sure when he was coming back. I'd only meant to put the file on his desk and leave, but I liked being in his office. Liked the hint of his cologne I could smell.

Still, I was being paid to work not sniff his lingering cologne. I bent and grabbed for the file that had slid partially beneath Dane's desk. Before I could straighten, a hand grabbed my hip and I made a squeak of surprise when I felt the now-familiar hardness against my ass.

"Hello, sweetheart."

I straightened but before I could move away, Mason's arm was wrapped around my waist. "Mason, we're at the office."

"We are," he said. I could hear the amusement in his voice as he cupped my breast and gave it a squeeze.

I glanced at the door to Dane's office as I placed my hand over Mason's.

"I closed it," Mason said before kissing the side of my throat. "And locked it."

I relaxed against his broad chest. I probably should have been encouraging distance at work, but I craved his touch and being close to him.

"How's your day going?" Mason asked.

"Good. Busy. Dane is at a meeting right now."

"I know." His fingers toyed with my nipple through my shirt. "He texted me."

"I should get back to work." I clamped my mouth shut against the moan when Mason rubbed his dick against my ass.

"In a minute. I have a gift for you."

"You do?" I turned around, smiling at the box in Mason's left hand. A pretty green ribbon was tied around it. "What is it?"

"You'll have to open it and find out," he said. "It's from me and Dane, actually."

"You guys didn't have to get me anything," I said. "You've already done so much for me."

"Open it, sweetheart." He kissed the tip of my nose and handed the box to me.

I untied the long silk ribbon and handed it to Mason to hold as I took off the lid and set it on the desk. I unfolded the green tissue paper and stared at the object before picking it up. "What is this?"

"It's a plug," Mason said with a small grin.

"A plug for what?"

His big hand squeezed my ass and understanding crashed into me. My cheeks turned pink, my nipples went hard, and my pussy was definitely getting wet. My immediate arousal was a little embarrassing. I'd been living with Dane and Mason for over a week now and I was seriously worried that I might be addicted to sex. I had sex with one or both every night and usually in the morning too, and I still couldn't get enough of either of them.

Sex with them was a drug and I was a hopeless addict.

"It's a butt plug." My voice was barely above a whisper.

"It is," Mason said.

"I don't think – I mean, am I ready for that?"

"You've had both mine and Dane's fingers in your ass the last couple of days," Mason said. "It's time to try the plug."

Pleasure and shame flooded through me. I'd

liked the feel of their fingers in my ass much more than I'd thought I would. I'd protested a little, but the second Mason's fingers had pushed past that tight ring of muscle, I'd been in heaven. Having fingers in my ass while being fucked only made my orgasm that much stronger.

Still, there was a difference between fingers and the plug that I was staring at. One end was a flat round jewel and the flared end of the plug seemed impossibly large. There was no way it was fitting in my butt.

"Um, it's a little big," I said. "And what's with the jewel?"

Mason grinned. "We want our girl to look pretty."

I touched the butt plug apprehensively. "I'm not ready for this."

"You are," Mason said. "You only need to wear it for a few hours, all right?"

I chewed on my bottom lip. "Okay."

"Good." His hand squeezed my ass again and then he reached into the box and pushed the tissue paper aside to reveal a small bottle of lube. "Turn around and bend over the desk, sweetheart."

My mouth dropped open, and Mason made a low growl of need. "Sweetheart, you know what happens when your mouth is open like that. You get a nice big cock to fill it."

I swallowed hard, suddenly wondering what it would be like to give Mason a blow job right here in the office.

Completely unprofessional, Naomi.

"I'm not wearing the plug right now," I said.

"Yes, you are," Mason said.

"I'll try it tonight at home."

"No," he said.

That one word made my pussy almost drip with anticipation. God, what was it about Mason and Dane dominating me that got me so hot? I didn't have a clue, but the last week had made it perfectly clear that, right or wrong, I loved it when they told me what to do in the bedroom.

You're not in the bedroom.

True, I wasn't, but the way Mason was looking at me, the way he was acting like it was a perfectly normal request for me to bend over Dane's desk and have a plug inserted in my ass, was making me weirdly hot.

"I can't wear this at work," I said. "What if someone finds out?"

"Considering that Dane and I are the only ones who get to see you naked, no one else is going to know," Mason said. "Turn around."

"I don't want to," I said.

His eyebrow arched and he said, "Turn around now, Naomi, or I'll spank you."

"You wouldn't," I said. I hadn't been spanked by either Mason or Dane yet. I'd been perfectly content to do everything they'd told me to do.

"I would," he said.

"But people would hear."

He laughed. "Sweetheart, I'll invite them in to watch if you keep sassing me the way you are."

I scowled at him and he took the plug from me. "Turn around and bend over the desk."

"Mason…"

"Do it." His tone was firm and unyielding, and more hot pleasure flooded through me. Without another word I turned and bent over Dane's desk until my breasts were pressed against it and my ass was up in the air.

Mason made a sound of appreciation and set the lube and the plug on the desk. "Hands behind your back, Naomi."

"What for?"

He slapped my ass hard and I cried out at the sting. My face flushed. If someone was walking by Dane's office, they would have heard it.

That's what you get for being a bad girl.

My pussy soaking wet now, I put my hands behind my back, my breath catching in my throat when I felt Mason loop the ribbon from my present around my wrists. He pulled it tight, wrapping it a few more times before tying it into a knot.

I tugged experimentally. Despite the thinness of the ribbon, there was no give to it at all and dark lust beat in my belly. I was helpless now and Mason would put the plug in my butt whether I wanted it or not.

That errant thought turned me on more than I wanted to admit. God, no wonder I never safe worded. I was ridiculously kinky.

The cool air kissed my ass cheeks as Mason eased my skirt up over my hips and bunched it around my waist.

"Look at you wearing a thong," Mason said. "Spread your legs, sweetheart."

I blushed but spread my thighs wide, feeling the strain in my lower calves as I rested my heated cheek on the desk below me. "I wanted to try wearing one, so I went shopping after work a couple days ago."

He traced the silk between my ass cheeks. "Do you like it?"

"It's all right," I said. "I'm not sure if it's my fav- oh!"

"Shh, sweetheart," Mason said as his fingers rubbed my pussy through the silk fabric again. "Not so loud. My God, you are so fucking wet, aren't you? You like being tied up and bent over Dane's desk."

"No, I don't," I said. "I don't like it... oh, oh God..."

Mason's fingers had slipped beneath my panties. He caressed my clit again before sliding two fingers deep into my pussy. I ground against his fingers as he fucked me, trying not to moan too loudly.

"You fucking love it, dirty girl." I could hear the amusement and lust mixed in Mason's voice. "Look at how wet you are."

He put his fingers in front of my face and I stared at the wetness on them before closing my eyes in embarrassment.

Mason traced his fingers across my lips. "Open and suck, Naomi."

I sucked his fingers clean as Mason rubbed my ass with his other hand.

"Good girl," he said. His fingers dipped back into my pussy, teasing and stroking and driving me crazy. "I could probably put this plug in without any lube, just use the wetness from your little pussy."

"Mason, please," I whimpered as he rubbed my clit with firm circles.

"Don't cum, Naomi," he said.

I muttered a curse under my breath, and he laughed before squeezing my ass. "Raise up a little."

I did what he asked, and he pulled my panties to the middle of my thighs. "Do you have any idea how pretty you look right now?" he said.

"Thank you, sir."

"You're welcome."

I pulled at my ribbon bond when Mason slid his finger down the crack of my ass. He laughed again as he watched me struggle. "You can't get free, sweetheart. Stop trying."

I automatically clenched when his finger rested against my anus and Mason squeezed my ass cheek again. "Nope, relax."

"I can't," I said as I clenched again.

"This is going to be a little cold," he said before he dripped lube over my hole. I squealed, clenching even harder as his finger rubbed the lube into my skin.

"Shh," he said. "It's just my finger. Relax."

I took a deep breath and made myself relax. I'd had his finger in my back hole before, it was no big deal. I arched my back at the pressure as Mason eased his finger past the tight ring of muscle.

"Good, sweetheart." His other hand rubbed my ass and thighs as he added a second finger. "You're doing very well."

I moaned in response. God, this was kind of

hot. Lying on Dane's desk, exposed with my hands tied while my coworkers could be walking down the hallway was turning me on in a way I'd never experienced before.

Mason removed his fingers and I whined in protest. I could hear the smile in his voice as he patted my ass. "I know, sweetheart. You want your hole filled. Give me a second."

I couldn't see him, but from the sounds, I knew he was putting lube on the plug. I immediately tensed up. I tried to keep doing some deep breathing, but in my head, I kept seeing the wide end of the plug. It was so big, there was no way it would ever fit inside of me."

"Sweetheart, stop tensing," Mason said. There was dull pressure against my asshole, and I clenched again, my ass cheeks practically slapping together.

"Naomi." Mason's voice was firm but this time I couldn't make myself obey him. I mean, was having a plug in my ass really something I wanted or -

We both heard the door open at the same time. My entire body froze, my mind screaming at me to do something, anything to cover my naked, lube covered ass. Before I could move, the door closed and Dane's deep voice said, "Seriously, Mason?"

I slumped against the desk, my lungs working overtime to drag air in as Mason said, "What? You agreed we should try the plug on her today."

"I meant tonight, after work." Dane joined us and he leaned down and pressed a kiss against my mouth. "Hello, baby."

"Hi, Dane," I said.

"I didn't want to wait," Mason said. "Besides, how hot is it knowing that she's sitting at her desk with a plug in her ass?"

"Dane, tell him he has to wait," I said.

"What's with this?" Dane tugged on the ribbon around my wrists.

"She was being a bad girl," Mason said.

"I wasn't," I said. "I wasn't being a bad girl, Dane."

"If you weren't, Mason wouldn't have tied your wrists together," Dane said. His big hand smoothed down my ass cheek and between my legs.

I moaned as he touched my clit and then finger fucked me for a few glorious seconds. "Jesus, she's wet."

"I know, right?" Mason said. "She is fucking loving this."

"I don't," I said. "I don't want the plug in my ass at work. Dane, tell Mason we should do this at home."

Dane's rough finger touched my anus and I squeaked and clenched my ass shut again, this time slamming my thighs together for good measure.

"Dane," Mason said. "A little help?"

"My pleasure," Dane said. He reached down and pulled my thighs open, hooking one leg around my right thigh as Mason hooked his leg around my other thigh. Dane's big hands grabbed my ass cheeks and pried them apart and just like that I was fully exposed and completely helpless.

"Look at her little pussy," Dane said. "She's dripping onto my desk, she's so wet."

I groaned with embarrassment as Mason pressed the plug against my anus. "I know."

He applied steady pressure and I tried to wiggle forward. Mason's heavy hand landed on the small of my back and Dane squeezed my ass cheeks hard. "Don't move, Naomi."

"It hurts," I whined as Mason pushed the plug deeper.

"Shh, breathe out and push back against the plug," he instructed.

"What? No way," I said. "I'm not...ow! Dane!"

He slapped my ass cheek again. "Do what Mason tells you."

I craned my head and pouted at him. "I don't like this, sir."

"You will," he said. "Push back, baby."

I pushed back against the plug, letting my breath out in a harsh rush. There was a pulsing point of pain and Mason made a grunt of satisfaction as the plug slid into my ass.

"Good," Mason said as Dane released my ass.

I tried to straighten, and Mason applied pressure to my lower back. "No. Stay there, sweetheart. Let us look at you."

I stayed where I was, embarrassment and lust mixing within me as Dane and Mason looked over my body.

"How does it feel?" Dane said.

"Weird. Full. Uncomfortable," I said.

"You'll get used to it," Mason said.

"Please, can I stand up now, sir?" I said.

"In a minute." Mason rubbed my lower back.

I moaned when fingers slipped between my legs and rubbed my pussy. I ground against the fingers again, the pressure and discomfort in my ass forgotten as Dane rubbed my clit.

"Dane," Mason said. "She doesn't deserve an orgasm."

"Yes, I do," I panted. "Please, sir, I want an orgasm."

Dane chuckled, the sound low and sexy. "She's about to sit for the next three hours with a butt plug in her ass while she enters the world's most boring data information. She deserves an orgasm." His fingers tugged at my clit, and I clamped my lips shut against the loud moan.

"Fine," Mason said. "But only one, and it needs to be quick, I have a meeting in five minutes."

"That's not going to be a problem," Dane said. "She's already about to cum."

I moaned in agreement, my bound hands clenching and unclenching in tight fists as I felt Mason's fingers slide into my pussy. He leaned over me, his other hand sliding under my head so he could press his hand across my mouth.

I appreciated the assist. Dane was right – I was about thirty seconds from cumming and there was no way I could be quiet about it.

Dane's fingers teased my clit as Mason fucked me hard with his fingers. Moaning and wiggling against Dane's desk, I wasn't even embarrassed by the wet sucking sounds my pussy made as it clung eagerly to Mason's fingers. Fifteen seconds later, I came screaming against Mason's hard palm, my pussy milking Mason's fingers and my ass clenching around the plug.

I collapsed against the desk, breathing hard as Mason and Dane rubbed my ass and thighs.

"Be right back," Mason murmured.

A few seconds later, a warm wet cloth was between my legs. I jerked, my sensitive clit protesting, but Dane kept me on the desk as Mason cleaned my pussy and then dried it with a towel. He pulled my panties up over my hips, placing the silk ribbon of fabric snug against the jeweled end of the plug in my ass.

Dane grabbed a pair of scissors from his desk and snipped the ribbon around my wrists free. He rubbed my wrists gently as Mason tugged my skirt down over my hips and ass.

"Stand up, baby," Dane said.

I struggled to do what he asked, swaying on my feet a little. Dane braced me against his large body and smoothed away from my face a few stray strands of hair that had fallen out of my braid. "You feel better, baby?"

"I feel really good," I said.

He smiled and kissed my mouth before rubbing my ass. "Good girl. Go back to your desk and do your work. I left the files on your desk."

"Yes, sir," I said.

I took a few steps, grimacing at the unfamiliar feel of the plug in my ass. "Do I really have to wear this?"

"Yes," Mason said. "We'll take it out for you when we get home tonight. Understand?"

"Yes, sir," I said.

He pressed a kiss against my mouth. "Have a

good afternoon, sweetheart."

"I have a plug in my butt," I grumbled. "How good is it gonna be?"

Mason and Dane both laughed, and I smiled at them before walking carefully from the office.

Chapter Eleven

Dane

"Fuck, that client is an asshole," Mason said as he met me in the driveway.

"Tell me about it." I slammed my car door shut, Mason locked his car, and we walked toward the house.

"Did you text Naomi?"

"Yeah," I said. "Told her we were on her way home."

"Poor girl. We would end up working late the day we put a plug in her ass," Mason said. "Maybe we should have told her to take it out. It's been almost six hours."

"We'll take it out before we eat dinner," I said, "and I'll eat her pussy to make it up to her."

"God, she has a sweet tasting pussy, doesn't she?" Mason said.

I nodded distractedly as I unlocked the front door. She really did and my mouth was already watering at the thought of burying my face between her thighs. I couldn't get enough of Naomi and I knew without a doubt that I wanted to spend the rest of my life with her.

Now I just needed to convince Mason and Naomi.

"Dane." Mason's hand rested on my arm before I could open the door.

"What?" I said impatiently.

"I know you're in love with Naomi."

"So what if I am?"

He shifted his laptop bag to his other hand. "Naomi is a sweet girl but she's a decade younger than us and she's spent her entire life living under her father's thumb. What she's doing with us is a... well, it's an experiment for her. You know that, right? She's not going to want to be with both of us for the rest of her life."

I could feel the muscle in my jaw ticking. "We're good to her and she likes us. Why wouldn't she want to stay?"

"Buddy." I hated the *get your fucking head out of the clouds* look that Mason was giving me. "She isn't serious about us. Does she like us? Sure, she does. But there's a big difference between like and love and what Naomi feels for us isn't -"

"It could be love," I said. "How the fuck would you know? You've never had a woman in love with you before."

"Dane," Mason said, "don't be a dick."

"Sorry," I muttered. "I'm just... I care about her a lot."

"I know you do." Mason clapped me on the back. "I do too. But she doesn't love us, and you need to be prepared that once she's gotten her fill of us, she's gonna move on."

Mason's matter-of-fact tone raised my hackles. "And you don't fucking care, do you?"

He grimaced and I saw a flash of pain in his eyes. "Fuck you, Dane. I'm not some cold-hearted bastard who -"

"I know." I wanted to punch the side of the house. Instead, I reached out and squeezed Mason's shoulder. "That was a shit thing for me to say and I'm sorry. But the thought of Naomi leaving us makes me wanna fucking puke. I'll go insane if she leaves, Mason."

"You won't," he said, but I could see the unease in his face. "Look, you need to take a step back, is all I'm saying, okay?"

"I can't," I said. "I love her, and I want us to be with her for the rest of our lives. You want that too."

"We barely know her," Mason said. "I'm not in love with her."

I snorted and reached for the door handle. "Hey, if it makes you feel better, keep lying to yourself and to me."

"Dane, I don't -"

"Enough," I said. "You said what you wanted to say, and I listened. Now, I want to be with Naomi. I *need* to be with her, and you do too. So, stop your fucking talking and let's get in there and give our woman some orgasms. If you'd stop trying to convince yourself that she's gonna leave, and instead work a little harder at making her cum, maybe we might have a chance at getting her to stay."

"Yeah, because the magic power of our dicks is gonna make her give up all her dreams and just be with us," Mason said with an epic eye roll.

"Fuck off," I said without malice. "Naomi can have her dreams *and* us, if you stop being such a fucking wet rag about everything."

I opened the door before he could reply and toed off my shoes then tossed my laptop bag on the side table. "Naomi? We're home!"

"Hey, I'm in the living room."

My heart sped up at just the sound of her voice and I almost jogged down the hallway. "Sorry, we're late, baby."

"That's fine." Naomi smiled up at me from the couch. She was curled up at the far end with her laptop balancing on her thighs. She'd changed into a t-shirt and yoga pants and my cock swelled at the way her bra-less tits pressed against the fabric.

Fuck, I couldn't wait to suck on her nipples.

"How did the meeting go?" she said.

"Client was an asshole." Mason walked into the living room, loosening his tie. "It's why we're so late. He wanted to go over his goddamn statements fifty fucking times."

"I'm sorry," Naomi said as I dropped onto the couch next to her.

I pressed a kiss against her mouth before glancing at her laptop. It was open to the homepage of one of our local colleges. "You set up a meeting with the dean at the college yet?"

"No, not yet. I was just looking at the program requirements again."

Mason leaned over the back of the couch, studying the laptop. "I thought this was your third-choice college. Why aren't you looking at your first choice?"

"Oh, uh, the first two don't offer the interior design program through night courses only so, you know..." Naomi cleared her throat. "Anyway, this college is still good and –"

"You should go to the school you want to go to," I said.

She just shrugged and closed her laptop. "I never even thought I'd get the chance to take interior design at a college, so I'm good with whatever."

I frowned at Mason. I wanted Naomi to have exactly what she wanted, and I hated that she was settling for her third choice. But she'd refused to even consider quitting working for me and going to school full time even when I'd offered to pay her tuition. I decided to try again.

"There is a way to go to your first-choice college," I said.

"I'm not quitting my job, Dane. I need it."

"You don't. You can continue to live here for free and -"

"Even without paying rent to you, I still need money for basic living expenses – my share of the groceries, personal stuff, clothes. My student loan will be much higher if I have to use it for living expenses as well," Naomi said. "If I'm still working, I can get a smaller student loan, one that only covers tuition."

A worried look crossed her beautiful face. "If I

even qualify for a student loan."

Annoyance was edging its way into my voice. "If you let me pay for your tuition like I offered before, you wouldn't have to worry about a student loan."

"No," she said. "Look, I appreciate that you want to help me, I really do, but I already owe you too much. I'm not paying any rent and the money you paid my father is -"

"Stop," Mason said. "We've told you before that you're not on the hook for the money we gave your father. We don't even care about that, okay? We just care that you're safe and away from your dickhead of an old man."

She took his hand and squeezed it. "I appreciate that, but I can't take any more 'gifts' from you. I just can't. Please try and understand."

I didn't understand, not one bit, but I didn't know how else to convince her that paying her tuition would be a drop in the bucket for me. Maybe if I showed her my bank account balance, she'd finally understand.

"A student loan isn't the best option," Mason said. "You'll be paying interest for years."

"I know," she said. "But I want to start my life and saving up for tuition will take too long. I don't want to be a secretary forever." She glanced at me and grimaced. "Not that I don't appreciate the job I have, I do, but I -"

"I get it," I said before stroking her long dark hair. "I just want you to be happy, baby."

She smiled and leaned over to press a kiss against my jaw. "I really appreciate that."

"How about a personal loan?" Mason said.

She shook her head. "The bank isn't going to give me a loan. I have no credit rating and I literally opened an account with them a week ago."

"Not from the bank, from us," Mason said.

Fuck, my best friend was brilliant.

"What?" Naomi stared at us.

"A loan from us," I said. "Our interest rate will be much lower."

I glanced at Mason, silent communication passing between us. There was no way in hell we'd ever make Naomi pay back a dime of the *loan*, but she didn't need to know that right now.

"A loan from you and Mason," Naomi said.

"Yes," Mason said. "Why not?"

"Because you'll probably do something adorable but incredibly annoying like refuse to take loan payments," Naomi said.

My face flushed. "We wouldn't do that."

"Bullshit," she said and then blushed.

I traced her warm cheeks. "Smart people curse more, Naomi."

She giggled. "Right. Anyway, if you promise that you'll actually let me pay you back, I'll consider a personal loan from the two of you for schooling."

"Sure, sure, we'll iron out the details later," Mason said before kissing the top of her head. "Did you eat?"

"No, I wanted to wait for the two of you," Naomi said.

"You shouldn't starve yourself," I said with a frown.

"Oh please." She laughed and patted her round tummy. "I can skip a couple of meals without worrying about starving."

"Naomi," Mason said warningly, "what did we say about talking shit about yourself?"

"I'm not," she said. "I'm just pointing out that during a zombie apocalypse, I'll be better equipped to survive than the two of you 'zero percent body fat' gods, because I have the reserves to go a few days without regular meals."

Mason burst out laughing and even I smiled as Naomi grinned at the two of us. "What is the dinner plan?"

"We'll grill something," I said, "but first, let's get the plug out of your ass so you're a bit more comfortable. Sorry you ended up wearing it for longer than we intended, but I'll make it up to you with a pussy eating."

"Oh, um," Naomi cleared her throat, "I took the plug out when I got home."

"Did you?" Mason raised his eyebrow at her. "Didn't we tell you we'd take it out when we got home?"

"Well, yeah, but…"

"But what?" I said. Dark pleasure was spearing through my belly. We hadn't spanked Naomi yet and I knew that Mason was just as eager to spank her as I was. But Naomi hadn't broken any rules and we'd had no reason to spank her. Until today.

"You were late," she said. "I didn't want to keep wearing it. It was starting to be uncomfortable."

"What did we say about the plug?" Mason said.

She flushed. "That you would take it out. But, sir, I -"

"You broke the rules, Naomi," I said. "What happens when you break the rules?"

Her cheeks were turning brighter, but it wasn't just anxiety that was bringing the colour to her cheeks. Nope, she was turned on... I could almost smell her arousal.

Mason's hand wound through her hair and he tugged her head back until she was staring up at him. "Answer him, Naomi."

I stared at her tits. Her nipples were protruding against the fabric of her t-shirt, and my cock hardened when Mason reached down with his free hand and lazily flicked one of her nipples. She gasped and jerked, her hands squeezing into tight fists. I set her laptop on the coffee table as Mason pressed a soft kiss on Naomi's mouth.

"Answer him, sweetheart."

"A spanking," Naomi whispered. "I get a spanking if I break the rules."

"That's right." I took her wrists. Mason released her hair and with one hard tug, I had her over my lap, her upper body resting against the couch and her lower half draped over my legs. My dick was digging into her stomach and her perfect ass was ready and ripe for a spanking.

I rubbed her ass through her yoga pants as she propped her elbows on the couch and lifted her body up a little. Her breathing was rapid, and her eyes were bright, and she was staring over her shoulder at me.

"What's your safe word, Naomi?" Mason said.

"Red." Her voice was high pitched and breathless.

"Good girl." Mason moved around the couch and curled his fingers around the waistband of her yoga pants.

When Naomi didn't move, I gave her a hard spank. "Hips up."

She squealed and lifted her hips up, her knees digging into the couch, her back arched and her ass sticking up in the air. Fuck, seeing her like this almost made me want to forget the spanking and just fuck her.

Almost.

Mason pulled on her pants and her panties, dragging both down her thighs. We stared at her ass. The paleness of her cheeks made me itch to cover it with my handprints. I couldn't wait to see it bright red. When we were finished with her, she'd know exactly who her ass and her pussy belonged to.

I smoothed my hand over Naomi's ass, smiling a little when she jumped and her flesh quivered under my hand. "Shh, baby," I said before giving one full cheek a squeeze.

"Sir," Naomi's voice was quivering too, "I don't want a spanking."

"Then you should have been our good girl," Mason said. He'd already stripped off his suit jacket and his tie and was unbuttoning his shirt.

"Okay, but you won't spank me like… hard-hard. Right?" Naomi was still staring at us over her shoulder.

I pressed on her lower back until she was lying

across my lap again. Her pants and underwear were still around her thighs and Mason tugged them all the way off before rubbing his dick through his pants.

"Are you-are you both spanking me, sir?" Naomi said.

"Just Dane this time," Mason said.

I felt Naomi relax a fraction against me. I knew what she was thinking. The last week had proven to her that I was a total fucking softie when it came to her. It was true – I had a hard time denying her what she wanted. If it wasn't for Mason, she'd have her orgasm the second she asked for it, be fucked the moment she batted those pretty blue eyes at us and asked us to give her a dick.

But, my smile widened as I rubbed my hand over her ass again, she'd never broken the rules before. She was about to find out what happened when she didn't obey us.

Mason was at Naomi's front now, and he pulled her t-shirt up and over her head, leaving her gloriously naked. She arched up on her elbows again, giving Mason access to her tits. He rubbed her nipples and she made little mewing sounds of pleasure, her pussy grinding against my thigh.

I smiled and rearranged her so that my right leg was over both of her thighs, pinning her against my lap and the couch. She peered over her shoulder at me as Mason continued to pet her tits. I knew she was confused as to why I pinned her down, but I just smiled at her and rubbed her lower back. "Look at Mason, baby."

She turned her head obediently to stare at

Mason. He smoothed her hair back from her face, I could see his hand trembling the tiniest bit, before rubbing her cheekbone with his thumb. "What's your safe word, sweetheart?"

"Red."

"Good." He pressed on the back of her head, guiding her face back down to the couch until her cheek was resting against the cushions. I'd been rubbing her lower back the entire time and I could tell any nervousness she'd been feeling was gone. She was confident I wouldn't spank her hard and like the bastard I was, I couldn't wait to prove her wrong.

I squeezed and kneaded her ass before slapping the right cheek. She squealed but there wasn't much heat behind my slap, and she giggled nervously before wiggling her ass at me. "Should I say thank you, sir?"

I growled under my breath at her cheekiness and slapped her left cheek. She didn't realize it, but these light slaps were nothing more than a way of getting her warmed up and preparing her ass for the actual spanking.

Without speaking I slapped her ass again, alternating cheeks until her butt was warm and a light rose colour. Mason unbuttoned his pants and pulled his dick out, rubbing it with rough strokes as he watched me paddle Naomi's ass.

Naomi's eyes were closed, a small and almost dreamy smile on her lips as she rubbed her little pussy against my rock-hard dick.

"How are you feeling, baby?" I rubbed her ass again.

"Good," she said. That dreamy smile turned impudent. "Maybe I should be a bad girl more often. Being spanked isn't so bad and I -"

I spanked her right cheek so hard, my hand tingled. Naomi jerked and squealed, rearing up from the couch, her beautiful tits bouncing as I gave her left cheek another hard spank. She immediately tried to wiggle away but her thighs were pinned beneath mine and she wasn't going anywhere.

I spanked her again as she cried out and her lower legs kicked uselessly in the air. "Dane, ow! Ow, that hurts! Stop it!"

I braced my hand on her lower back and spanked her right in the middle of both cheeks. She shrieked and tried to push my hand away when I rubbed her ass. "Ouch! Dane, ouch!"

I spanked her again. "Baby, every time you call me Dane, I add another five spanks to your punishment."

She glared at me, her eyes spitting sparks and her teeth bared. "Stop it, *sir*!"

"Better," I said, "but two spanks added for thinking you can tell me what to do."

She shrieked in outrage when I gave her two hard spanks. She flailed her hands behind her body, trying to smack me on the arm and chest.

"Mason," I said.

He leaned over the arm of the couch, his dick practically in Naomi's face, and grabbed her arms, yanking them up until they were stretched above her head with her hands gripping the arm of the couch. She struggled furiously against his grip and yelled out a few choice curse words when I spanked her hard five times in a row.

Her ass was bright red now and seeing my handprints on her skin made my cock so fucking hard, I could barely think straight. I rubbed my fingers back and forth over the backs of her thighs before squeezing her ass.

"Let me go, Mason!" she shouted.

I spanked her five more times and she wailed loudly. "I mean, sir! Let me go, sir!"

Tears were starting to slide down her cheeks and her body was trembling. She hadn't safe worded and I was impressed with and proud of our girl. I slid my hand between her legs, smiling when her back arched. Her pussy was soaking wet and I rubbed her clit as a reward and to soothe her. Her body shuddered and she moaned happily as I circled her clit and gave it a firm pinch.

"Oh, oh yes," she moaned, her thighs relaxing under mine and spreading apart. "Oh God, that feels so good."

I slid a finger into her pussy, smiling again when her inner muscles clamped around me. "You're so wet, baby. You're enjoying your spanking."

"No, I'm not," she said. "I don't like it at... oh God, oh fuck, that's so good."

I was thumbing her clit with a hard and circular motion and she ground her pelvis against me. She was already on the verge of her orgasm, the spanking, the finger fucking, and being held down by Mason had her all worked up.

I pulled my hand free of her clit and she kicked her feet in protest, her head whipping around to stare at me. "Sir, no!"

"Shh, baby," I said before slapping her ass.

She squealed, her feet kicking again and her entire body wiggling as she tried to get free of mine and Mason's grip.

"Only five more," I said.

"I can't!" she wailed. "Please, sir, it hurts."

"I know," I said and spanked her again.

Her temper got the best of her and she turned her head to glare at me. "You're the worst! You're so mean!"

I rubbed her ass. It was hot to the touch and I reveled in that heat as I grinned and said, "Keep spouting off like that, baby, and your mouth's gonna be filled with Mason's cock while I finish your spanking."

Her glare turned into a pout and I studied the tears on her cheek. I was lying about the cock sucking. She needed to be able to speak in case she safe worded, but I had a feeling that she'd like it if we made her suck dick while being spanked.

I filed that away for a future spanking and then slapped her ass nice and hard. She cried out and I said, "Are you going to be our good girl, Naomi? Are you going to obey us from now on?"

She didn't reply and I spanked her twice more. She muttered a curse, more tears sliding down her cheeks. "Yes, sir! I'll behave! I promise!"

"Good girl," I said and gave her one final spank.

She jerked and cried out, slumping against the couch when I moved my leg off of hers. She buried her face in the couch, her body hitching as she cried softly. I would have felt sorry for her if the huge wet spot on my pants hadn't told me exactly how much she enjoyed her spanking.

Mason was already taking off his pants and I quickly stood and stripped out of my clothes. I didn't have a condom on me, but I'd fuck her bareback and then pull out and cum on the smooth red flesh of her ass.

"Baby, on your hands and knees," I said. "It's time for your reward."

"I don't want a reward," her voice was muffled against the couch. "I want to go upstairs to my room and think about how much the both of you suck."

I bellowed laughter and Naomi climbed to her knees and glared at me. "That really hurt, Dane. I didn't like the spanking."

"Oh yeah? Because your little pussy is dripping. I can see your sweet cream all over your inner thighs."

Her face flushed and she made a little squeak when I pushed her down on the couch with her hands gripping the arm of the couch. I kneeled behind her, gently rubbing her sore ass. "I'm going to fuck you now, baby, and you're going to suck on Mason's cock. Understand?"

"Yes, sir,' she said.

"I don't have a condom, but I'll pull out before I cum. You all right with that?"

She nodded and I loved her trust in me. As much as I wanted to put a baby in Naomi, I would never do it without her permission.

I knelt on the couch behind her as Mason pressed up against the arm of the couch. He scooped her hair into a ponytail and gripped the base of his dick with his other hand, guiding it to her mouth. "Open, sweetheart."

She opened, taking in his cock with eager enthusiasm. She was already better at cock sucking. Our girl was a fast learner, and I loved how open and willing she was to give us pleasure.

I pressed the head of my fat cock against her clit and rubbed back and forth, loving the way she squealed around Mason's dick and tried to grind against me.

I gave her what she wanted, sinking my cock into her tight, hot pussy. She was so wet, I slid in easily, despite the way she tried to grip me with her inner muscles. When I was balls deep, I held her hips. She moaned when my pelvis brushed against her red ass and I stroked her lower back.

"I know, baby, it hurts your little ass, but we'll take care of that after you've been fucked."

She squeezed her pussy around me in reply and I groaned loudly and made three harsh thrusts. I'd lost track of how many times I'd fucked Naomi now, but her little pussy still made me want to cum in three seconds flat.

I gritted my teeth and watched as she sucked Mason's cock before I started a slow and deep rhythm. I reached beneath her and wetted my thumb with the liquid that coated her pussy before working it into her ass. She clenched and moaned, her tight hole was probably a little on the sore side from having the plug in it, and I rubbed her hip.

"No, baby, let me in. Give me what I want or it's another spanking."

I was lying. We wouldn't spank her again, not for a few days at least, but I liked the way she submitted immediately. Her ass relaxed and I pushed my thumb past that tight ring of muscle before fucking her hard and fast, nearly shoving her face into Mason's cock.

We got a pretty good rhythm going and I groaned and let my head fall back. I figured I had maybe another minute, minute and a half tops, before I blew my load. I reached under Naomi again with my free hand and found her hard little pearl of a clit. The minute I started to rub it her climax exploded within her. Her beautiful body tensed, and she screamed around Mason's cock as she came.

Her pussy milked me hard and I was beyond tempted to cum deep inside of her. Instead, I pulled out and rubbed my dick hard, letting my orgasm wash over me as I coated Naomi's ass and lower back with my hot cum. I moaned when I lifted my gaze to Mason and realized he had pulled out of Naomi's mouth and was cumming all over her tits. My cock twitched in my hand, more cum spilling out to land on her perfect ass.

I rubbed it into her skin, breathing harshly. Mason was rubbing his cum into Naomi's tits as she trembled on her hands and knees, her breath rushing in and out of her lungs, and her eyes closed tight.

I squeezed her hip. "Okay, baby?"

Mason leaned down and kissed her forehead, his touch gentle as he rubbed her upper back. "Are you all right, sweetheart?"

A smile curved Naomi's lips. "I came so hard.

I've never cum that hard before."

I laughed and patted her thigh. "That's good, baby. Come on, let's get you in the shower and then we'll cook you dinner."

Chapter Twelve

Naomi

"Crap." I stopped and adjusted the strap on my sandal, trying to balance on one foot as I did so. The heels were low, but after wearing flats for most of my life, I was still trying to get used to walking in even these low heels.

I smiled as I straightened and continued down the sidewalk toward the café near our office building. I loved my new clothes and shoes. I loved that I could wear makeup without worrying about getting in trouble. I loved that every penny of my paycheque went directly to a bank account that belonged to me and only me, and I especially loved fucking Mason and Dane every day.

I waited a beat, pleased with myself when my face didn't flush bright red. I was getting better at not being so stupidly shy about sex. Hell, yesterday morning before work, Dane had put the plug in my ass, and I'd worn it until lunch time without even really thinking about it. It was surprising how normal it felt after only a few days of wearing a butt plug.

Mason and Dane made me wear a plug every time we had sex now and to my surprise, it was incredibly enjoyable. Just having it wiggled while it was in me, made my orgasm incredibly powerful, and I'd found myself daydreaming the last day or two about what it would be like to actually have a dick in my ass.

This time I did flush a little, but could you blame me? I was thinking about having sex with two men at once and I was pretty sure that porn aside, most women didn't do that.

Whore.

I ignored my inner voice. It was becoming easier and easier every day to ignore it. In fact, I didn't really believe it anymore. Maybe what Dane and Mason and I had wasn't conventional, but it didn't make me a whore either.

What you have? Girl, you don't have anything with them. Sure, they're enjoying banging your brains out, but that won't last forever. You need to start looking for your own place and get used to the idea of living on your own. Once they tire of you, they're not gonna want you to keep living with them. I don't care what they say.

I winced, my steps slowing until I was at a standstill in the middle of the sidewalk. The lunch crowd dodged around me and I heard a few impatient grunts and sighs of annoyance, but I didn't move. The thought that Dane and Mason would one day be tired of me, sent dismay spiraling through me.

I didn't want them to be tired of me. I loved them and I wanted to spend the rest of my life with them.

Oh, girl, you idiot.

Yeah, probably. But I couldn't help the way I felt. I hadn't planned on falling in love with two men but that didn't negate the fact that I was. Only, it meant being alone the rest of my life once they were finished with me.

I started walking again. Maybe they didn't love me, but that didn't mean I just had to give up without a fight. I'd spent most of my life being cowed by my father, never getting what I wanted, never having the power to make my own decisions, and I was over it. I loved Dane and Mason, I wanted to be with both of them, and I was gonna make that happen.

How hard could it be to make two guys fall in love with you?

I almost laughed out loud as I opened the café door and ducked inside. If you'd told me two months ago that I'd be having sex with two men and I'd be plotting a way to make both of them fall in love with me, I would have called you bonkers. It was funny how life had a way of –

"Naomi?"

I whirled around, my stomach dropping as I stared at my mother. "What are you doing here?"

"Please, honey, can we just talk?"

I hesitated. My mother was dressed like she was always dressed, a skirt to her ankles, a shirt that buttoned to her neck, and her hair in its usual bun, but she looked older and somehow... smaller. I realized that I'd never seen her without my father at her side before.

"Where is he?" I said before looking around the café.

"Not here," my mother said. "He doesn't know I'm here."

"Bullshit," I said.

My mother winced but didn't say anything about my foul language. "He doesn't. I've been sitting in the car outside your office building, hoping you might go for a walk at lunch or… or get a bite to eat. Please, can I join you? Just for a few minutes?"

I hesitated and then nodded. "But we're not talking about me coming home. That's not happening, ever."

"I know," she said. "I just wanted to see you again. I miss you, Naomi."

"Go and sit down, I'll grab us some food."

A few minutes later, I joined her at the table. I handed her a sandwich and a bottle of water before biting into my own sandwich.

We ate silently for a few minutes before Mom smiled tentatively at me. "This is good."

"The food is really good here," I said.

"You look good," she said. "Thinner."

I dropped my sandwich on the plate and grabbed my bottle of water. "That's all that matters, huh? That I'm thin?"

"No, honey, I didn't mean… that is…"

My mother looked so heartbroken that I couldn't help but thaw a little. "I know, Mom. I look good because I'm happy. And I'm happy because I'm not living under Dad's rule anymore. It's as simple as that."

"I'm sorry," she said. Tears were starting to slide down her cheeks and she pushed her sandwich away. "I'm so sorry, Naomi. What your father did was wrong, and I'm so sorry I let him do it. I should never have allowed that to happen."

"No, you shouldn't have. What he tried to do to me and what he did to Joy isn't right, and you let it happen."

Her face turned the shade of old curd and I could see the hurt in her eyes. My anger with her dissipated. She was as much a victim of my father's cruelty as Joy and I were.

"Mom, you don't have to stay with him," I said. "You can be free too. All of us can be free. We can get Joy back and we can find our own place and -"

"I can't leave your father," she said. "We've been married for nearly twenty-five years and I love him."

I grimaced. "You still love him after what he did to your children?"

"You can't help who you love," she said. "He tries to be a good man, he does. But he's weak. Satan has taken hold of him, but I promise he's fighting. He feels real remorse for what he did to you."

"Does he? Because I don't see him here asking for my forgiveness. I don't see him rescuing Joy from that horrible man he forced her to marry," I said.

My mother looked sick to her stomach but this time I didn't feel an ounce of sympathy for her.

Truthfully, I felt a little sick myself over my whiplash of emotions. I wanted to hate my mother, but I couldn't.

"I should get back to the office," I said.

"Honey, wait." She reached out and grabbed my hand. "I know you don't want to have anything to do with your father, but will you at least consider a relationship with me? I've already lost one daughter. I don't want to lose another."

"You let it happen," I said. "You let him send Joy away and -"

"I had no choice!" My mother's voice was loud enough that the couple sitting at the table next to us glanced over. "You don't understand what it's like to be married to someone like your father and I pray you never will. I miss Joy as much as you do, and I know what happened to her is my fault."

She started to cry, silent sobs that shook her entire body. My anger dissolved again into pity. "It isn't your fault, Mom. It's his. He did this to all of us."

"He isn't a monster," she whispered.

Sick and exhausted by the games, I said, "He is, and we both know it."

She studied our clasped hands before using some tissues from her purse to wipe her face. "I don't want to lose you too, Naomi."

"You won't. But I won't have anything to do with him. Do you understand? I'm willing to try and have a relationship with you, but only if he stays out of it."

"All right," she said.

"I mean it, Mom," I said. "If he tries to weasel

his way into my life by using you, I'll cut you both out of my life for good. Do you understand?"

"I do," she whispered.

For a moment, I was tempted to ask her if my father had blown all of the money from Mason and Dane while in Vegas, before letting it go. In the end, it didn't matter to me what he did with the money.

"I need to get back to work," I said. "I'll text you, okay?"

"How? Your father cancelled your phone plan." Her face flushed. "I begged him not to, said you wouldn't be able to get a hold of us, but he didn't, I mean…"

"He didn't care," I said. "Yeah, I'm not surprised. I have a new phone and my own plan now. I also have a bank account, a wardrobe that fits, and a friend named Jemma. I'm not the person I was even a month ago, Mom."

"I know," she said. "I'm happy for you, honey. Truly, I am."

I drank the rest of my water. "I'll text you."

"Do they treat you well?" she asked in a low voice. "The men who…"

"The men who saved me from being raped by that toad of a man, Deacon Dennison?" I said.

She flinched again but nodded.

"Yeah. They do. They're amazing people. They treat me with respect and kindness, and they don't expect or ask for blind obedience. Anything we do together is because I want it to happen."

"Naomi," my mother's voice was so low I had to strain to hear it, "are you – are you sleeping with them?"

"That's none of your business," I said. "I have to go. I'll text you in a couple of days, okay?"

"Okay," she said. "I love you, Naomi."

"I know. Talk to you soon, Mom."

৯ ৩

Mason

"Considering it's your birthday, you're in one hell of a mood." Dane clapped me on the back before sinking down on the couch beside me. "What's up?"

"Nothing," I said before downing the last of my whiskey in one burn-inducing swallow. "Where's Naomi?"

Dane shrugged. "Dunno. She said she had an errand to run after work but that she wouldn't be long. Hey, are you okay?"

I tried to school my face into something that resembled my normal mood. Not that it mattered. Dane had been my best friend for years, trying to hide my sudden melancholy from him was impossible.

"Dude, tell me what's wrong," Dane said.

I stared at my empty whiskey glass. Telling Dane that I'd realized this morning in the shower that I loved Naomi as much as he did felt risky. If I told him, he'd want us both to tell Naomi and I was positive she wasn't ready for that. If we told her how we felt, she'd freak out and leave, and both Dane and I would lose our goddamn minds.

I wished like fuck I hadn't let Naomi join me in

the shower this morning. She'd wanted to do something special for my birthday, she said, and apparently that meant giving me the world's most fucking incredible blow job in the shower. I honestly didn't know if she'd just improved her oral techniques that much in such a short time or if my love for her made me believe everything she did was incredible.

Either way, shortly after I'd cum in her mouth and then made her cum on my fingers, I'd realized that she was the one for me. I almost snorted out loud. It seemed like such stupid timing for a realization of love, but watching Naomi moan and writhe on my fingers as she climaxed, had brought any doubt or confusion into crystal clearness for me. Sweet, loving Naomi was the only woman I wanted for the rest of my life and there was no denying it.

"Mason?"

"I love her," I blurted out and then jumped up to refill my glass. I drank the whiskey in three swallows, my esophagus burning. "I fucking love her."

I glanced over at Dane who was staring at me with an amused look on his face. He raised his glass. "Congratulations on finally coming to your senses."

"We can't tell her," I said.

Dane frowned. "Why the fuck not?"

"She's not ready to hear that we love her. If we tell her that, if we tell her we want her to be with us the rest of her life, she'll cut and run, Dane."

"You don't know that she'll run," Dane said but

I could hear the doubt in his voice.

"You don't know that she won't. Look, we haven't known her that long, all right? We need to take this slow. We need to show her that she belongs with us by giving her time and her own space."

"That sounds like the opposite of what we should do," Dane said.

"Maybe with other women, but Naomi is unique," I said. "With her background and the way her father controlled her life, that's the very last thing we can ever do to her. If we tell her that we love her and want her to be with us permanently after less than two months of a relationship, she might think we're trying to control her."

"She won't," Dane said. "She knows us better than that."

"Maybe, but she hasn't lived much of a life until now. We're the only guys she's slept with and," I hated to say it, but it needed to be said, "she may want to... experiment with other guys. How many women do you know in this day and age who are happy to spend the rest of their life with the first guy they slept with?"

Dane's face looked like I'd just slammed his finger in a car door. I hated upsetting him, but he needed to keep a clear head about this. If he didn't, we might lose Naomi forever.

"Look, all I'm saying is that for now, we keep our true feelings to ourselves. We give Naomi a few more months of being with us, give her the opportunity to fall in love with us, and then we calmly and logically explain that we love her and want to spend the rest of our lives together."

"And if she decides to leave between now and then?" Dane said. "Then what do we do?"

"We let her go," I said.

His hand clenched around his whiskey glass. "No fucking way."

"If she doesn't want to be with us, we have to accept it." My voice was calm, but my insides were like two rats fighting over a crust of bread. If Naomi left us…

She won't. Just don't push her too hard and she won't.

"It'll be fine," I said. "There's still a lot we can teach her sexually, and if that's all that's keeping her tied to us at the moment, then we can use that to our advantage, right? We keep her completely happy with orgasms whenever she wants and also show her how much she means to us and how much we love her."

"Do you really think she's only with us because of the sex?" Dane said.

"Well, we know it's not our goddamn money. It's like pulling teeth to get her to accept any gifts from us. She still hasn't even agreed to let us give her the loan for her schooling and it's been almost two weeks since we offered."

Dane grimaced. "I'm seriously just gonna show her my goddamn bank account. Maybe then she'll realize that paying her tuition isn't a big deal."

"It's a big deal to her," I said. "Keep your fat bank account numbers to yourself. We can't push her into anything, Dane. Remember that. If she even thinks we're trying to control her like her father did, then we're fucked."

Dane drained the rest of his whiskey. "Jesus, now I'm in as bad of a mood as you are."

"Sorry," I said.

"Some fucking birthday this is turning out to be for you, huh?" Dane said.

"It's a good day," I said. "Any day spent with the woman I love and my best friend is a good day."

The front door opened and slammed shut and I could almost feel the gloom in the room lifting. Dane stood and, leaving his glass on the coffee table, jogged out of the living room.

I followed slowly, still feeling unsettled and anxious. Keeping my real feelings for Naomi hidden would be incredibly difficult. I already wanted to shout it from the fucking rooftops. I took a deep breath and stared at Dane when he stood in the doorway of the kitchen and blocked me from entering.

"What?"

Dane grinned at me. "Just wait a minute."

"Wait a minute for what?"

"I have a surprise for you," Naomi said from inside the kitchen. "Oh shit... ouch!"

"You okay, baby?" Dane said.

"Yeah, just incompetent with... uh, never mind."

"What's going on in there?" I said.

Dane's grin widened but he didn't reply. After about two minutes, Naomi said, "Okay, Dane let him in."

Dane retreated into the kitchen and stepped to the left. I stared at Naomi standing next to the island. A birthday cake, the candles on top blazing brightly, sat on the marble surface.

She smiled at me and started to sing. Dane joined in and a smile spread across my face. Neither Dane nor Naomi could carry a tune in a goddamn bucket, and it was, without a doubt, the worst rendition of 'Happy Birthday', I'd ever heard.

The song ended and Naomi said, "Make a wish and blow out your candles, birthday boy."

I closed my eyes, wished for Naomi's love, and blew out the candles. Naomi clapped her hands before hugging me and pressing a kiss against my mouth. I returned her kiss, reaching down to squeeze her ass. She giggled and pulled away. "Behave. You need to eat your cake first, then I have a present to give you."

"You didn't have to get me a present," I said.

She just smiled and handed the knife to me. "Cut the cake."

She removed the candles as Dane grabbed plates and cutlery.

"Did you guys eat yet?" Naomi asked.

"Nah, we were waiting for you," Dane said.

I cut into the cake as Naomi laughed and said, "Cake isn't the best birthday dinner. Sorry, Mason."

I grinned at her and tipped a piece onto her plate before handing it to her. "It's perfect."

"We could go out for dinner," Dane said before popping a large bite of cake into his mouth. "It's still early."

"I'm good with staying in," I said.

"We could order in some food from your

favourite restaurant," Naomi said.

"Sure." I ate a piece of cake. "This is delicious. Thank you, sweetheart."

"You're welcome." Naomi beamed at me. "I picked it up at this new bakery not far from the office. I wanted to bake you a cake but, honestly? I'm a decent cook but terrible at baking. Everything I try to bake turns out awful."

"I would have loved it anyway," I said.

She laughed. "You wouldn't. Trust me."

As she ate her cake, I couldn't stop staring at her. I wasn't the only one. Dane was studying her like a lovesick puppy, and I'm pretty sure I had the same stupid grin on my face. I couldn't help it. She was just so fucking pure and beautiful. I couldn't imagine my life without her. Didn't *want* to imagine it.

"Here, I'll take your plate," Dane said when Naomi was finished.

She handed him her plate and he took mine as well. He loaded the dishwasher as I moved to Naomi and put my arms around her waist. I pressed a kiss against her lips. She tasted sweet like the frosting, and she opened her mouth when I licked along her bottom lip. I took the kiss deeper, the sweetness of her mouth overwhelming me. When I finally pulled back, Naomi was breathless, and I had one hell of an erection.

Dane was leaning against the counter, arms folded across his chest, his erection pushing against his pants. Naomi smiled at me. "So, do you want your present first or do you want to order in dinner first?"

"Present," I said. I had no idea what the gift was, but I couldn't wait to see it. The idea that I would have something from Naomi, in case she decided to move on and we never saw her again, was weirdly soothing.

"Well," Naomi took a deep breath and glanced at Dane, "it's kind of an unconventional gift but I'm pretty sure you'll like it."

"I'll love it." I kissed her smooth throat. "Whatever it is, sweetheart."

"Okay, well, I thought for your birthday it would be nice if I, um, had sex with both of you. At once," she added hastily when neither Dane nor I said anything.

Beside us, Dane's body had gone stiff and he was staring at Naomi like, if he moved or said anything, she might change her mind. I didn't blame him. Naomi was offering us our biggest fucking fantasy and my cock was suddenly leaking so much precum, it was like a damn lake in my pants.

"Uh, if that's what you want." Naomi's voice was suddenly unsure. "I mean, if you don't, that's fine too. I could give you another blowjob for your birthday present instead."

I wanted to say something, anything, but I was struck dumb by the image of Naomi's lush body between mine and my best friend's. Of her being impaled on both of our dicks, of her moaning and wiggling and cumming while we fucked her hard.

"Can one of you say something?" Naomi said. "I thought the end goal was for all of us to have sex together, but you guys are starting to freak me out a little. Do you not want that?"

"Baby," Dane's voice was a hoarse rasp, "you have no fucking idea how much we want that."

"Then why are you acting so weird?" Naomi said.

"I don't know about Dane, but I don't have enough blood left in my brain to form coherent thoughts," I said.

Naomi laughed before reaching down and cupping my erection. "Your cock does seem to like the idea."

Jesus, I loved it when Naomi talked dirty. She'd been so shy when we'd first met her. I loved her newfound confidence about sex.

She reached out with her other hand to cup Dane's dick. As she rubbed and massaged both of us, she gave us a naughty smile. "What do you say we go up to the bedroom?"

"Fuck, yes."

Chapter Thirteen

Naomi

Dane and Mason hustled me upstairs to the bedroom, stripped me naked, and put my collar and cuffs on so fast, I almost giggled. I wondered if they thought I would change my mind. They were worrying needlessly if they did.

I wanted the both of them at once with an all-consuming need that wouldn't go away. The last few days, I'd been obsessed with the idea of fucking the two of them together and Mason's birthday was perfect timing.

Mason and Dane were stripping off their clothes. I watched with what I was sure was a dumb smile on my face as Dane took out lube and a condom from the drawer and set them both on the bedside table.

Mason sat next to me on the bed and took my hand. "Sweetheart, are you sure this is what you want? I love this as a birthday gift but if you're not ready or -"

"I'm ready," I said. "I want this more than anything, Mason."

Some of the tension left his shoulders as Dane sat on the other side of me and kissed my throat just above my collar. "You're so beautiful, Naomi."

"Thank you," I said. "You guys are beautiful too."

Mason cupped my breast, his fingers working my nipple into an aching hardness. "What you're doing tonight, what you're giving us, is an incredible gift, Naomi. Thank you."

I smiled at him. I loved how sweet and appreciative they were being, but holy God, if we didn't get to the fucking soon, I was gonna lose my mind.

"You're welcome. Now, can we get to the fucking?"

My face went hot at my words but both Mason and Dane laughed before Dane gave me a searing hot kiss that only flamed my need. "Yes, baby, we can get to the fucking. Lie on your back in the center of the bed and spread those beautiful thighs."

I did what he asked, frowning a little when he stretched out on his stomach between them. "This isn't a sex position, this is an... ohhh, oh right there."

Dane had licked my pussy from my entrance to my clit and I reached down and gripped his head, grinding my pussy against his mouth, even as I said, "We're supposed to be having sex, not... oh! Oh fuck!"

My body quivered and my complaint died in my throat when Dane sucked on my already throbbing clit. Dane was a master at eating pussy, and who was I to complain if he wanted to eat me out?

Mason was gently shoving pillows under my head and upper back. When he had me in the position he wanted, he tugged on the collar around my neck before trailing his fingers between my breasts and then pulling on my nipples.

I arched, staring hungrily at his dripping cock as Dane slid two fingers deep into my pussy.

"Open," Mason said with another tug on my collar.

I opened immediately, moaning happily when Mason slid his cock deep into my mouth. My cries of pleasure as Dane sucked on my clit again were muffled by Mason's thick shaft. I tried to concentrate on licking and sucking his dick, but Dane was going to town on my pussy and the pleasure was short-circuiting my brain.

I didn't know if it was the knowledge that I was about to be fucked by both of them, or if Dane was just putting extra effort into eating my pussy, but it took approximately three minutes before I was cumming all over his face. Mason's dick was still shoved deep into my mouth and he groaned when I sucked his dick frantically as I came.

He slid in and out of my mouth, his hands threaded deep in my hair as Dane sat up and wiped his face on the sheet. I was so wet I could feel my cream dripping down my pussy and into the crack of my ass. Dane was rolling on a condom and Mason pulled out of my mouth.

"You don't want her mouth first?" he said to Dane.

"No." Dane's big body was vibrating lightly. "I need to fuck her, Mason."

"You and me both," Mason said before sitting me up. "Move over, sweetheart. Let Dane lie down."

I moved to the side, closer to Mason, and he groaned again when I licked a path from his navel to his cock. I cleaned the precum from the head of his dick before kissing my way down his thick shaft. I was about to suck on his balls – I'd learned quickly that it drove him crazy when I did that – when he pulled me away from his dick with a hand around my collar.

"Mason, let me!" I scowled at him as he smoothed my hair back from my face.

"No, sweetheart. I'm already close to cumming."

I tugged free of his grip and tried to do it anyway. Mason pulled me away again and Dane gave me a sharp and painful slap to my ass.

I squealed and glared at both men. "Stop it."

"Be our good girl or I'll spank your ass before I fuck it," Mason said.

I shivered all over as I contemplated his words. Since my very first spanking, I'd been spanked twice more, once by Mason and once by Dane. Each time I'd both loved and hated it. It hurt like hell and sitting for the next few days was pure torture, but my orgasms after being spanked were off-the-charts intense. I had no idea what it was about being spanked that made me so hot, but despite knowing what the pain would be afterwards, I was seriously considering whether I wanted to disobey Mason.

Dane grinned and nipped at the back of my shoulder. "Do you have any idea how much I love that you enjoy being spanked?"

"I don't enjoy it," I lied.

Dane smacked my ass again, making me cry out and jerk forward. His hand cupped my throat and he pulled me back against his chest, his lips sucking at my earlobe and his fingers plucking at my right nipple. "Now you're lying to us? You really do want to be spanked. Don't you, bad girl?"

"What I want," I arched into Dane's touch, "is for the both of you to stop stalling and fuck me already."

Mason laughed and reached for the lube. "I thought it was my birthday present. Shouldn't I get to be the demanding one?"

Before I could reply, Dane had rolled to his back and was tugging on my collar. "C'mon, bad girl, ride my cock."

I climbed onto him eagerly. Any shyness about my extra weight had disappeared a long time ago. It was impossible not to know that Dane and Mason found me attractive and hot. You could see it in the way they looked at me, in the way they touched me. God, I loved them.

I straddled Dane, reaching down to grip his cock in my hand before sliding it into my soaking wet pussy. I groaned, his thickness filling me up and stretching my walls, just like it always did. It took a few tries before he was fully sheathed. Mason was stroking my back with the tips of his fingers, his cock already shiny with lube, and Dane smiled at me when I sank down fully and made another low groan.

"Good, baby?"

"Really good," I panted as I made a few short thrusts. Dane stayed perfectly still, letting me ride his cock the way I wanted as Mason continued to trace my back. When his lube-slicked fingers slipped between my ass cheeks and probed at my anus, I took a deep breath and relaxed.

"Good girl," Mason said before sliding two fingers deep into my ass.

As always, it felt surprisingly good, and I didn't resist when Dane reached up, curled his fingers around my collar and tugged me down until my breasts were pressed against his chest.

He kissed the tip of my nose, my chin, and then finally my mouth. I moaned and kissed him hard, sliding my tongue between his lips. His heavy arms curled around my waist and his hands rested in the small of my back as he pumped in and out of my pussy with hard and heavy strokes.

I moaned again, the combination of Mason's fingers in my ass and Dane's dick in my pussy, bringing me closer to an orgasm.

"Don't hold back, sweetheart," Mason said. "Cum for us."

I let my climax wash over me in a sweet, dizzying rush that made my pussy and my ass tighten around Dane's cock and Mason's fingers.

"It feels so good when you cum on my dick," Dane said against my mouth. Behind me, I could feel Mason moving into position between Dane's legs. I rested my forehead against Dane's and drew in a shuddering breath as the last of my climax made my entire body tingle.

Dane's big hands were gripping my ass and I jerked when he spread the cheeks apart and lube dripped over my hole.

"Shh, baby," he said and nuzzled my neck. "Just relax."

"Cold," I said.

"Sorry, sweetheart." Mason's fingers quickly warmed the lube up. "Are you ready for me?"

"I think so," I said.

"If you've changed your mind, it's okay," Mason said. "We can stop right now. Right, Dane?"

Dane laugh was a bit strangled. "Yeah, of course."

"I don't want to stop, and I haven't changed my mind," I said. "Do it, Mason."

The head of his cock pressed against me and Dane squeezed my ass cheeks before holding them open even wider.

"Deep breath, sweetheart," Mason said.

I breathed in deep and released it as Mason pushed. I pushed back against the pressure, telling myself not to freak out, that it wasn't any different from the plugs we'd been using.

Only it was different. Mason's cock was bigger than the plugs and the pressure was already feeling like too much. I gritted my teeth, blew out my breath and pushed back again. I was doing this even if it…

"Oh!"

The pop of pain made my eyes water and Dane

immediately released my ass and rubbed my lower back with his warm hands. "Deep breaths, baby. C'mon."

I sucked in air and let it out, before taking another breath and releasing it a bit more slowly.

"Okay?" Dane said.

"Yeah." The pain had vanished, and I was left with a feeling of unbelievable fullness.

I glanced over my shoulder at Mason. "Are you in?"

"The head is." He stroked my thighs.

"Just the head? Crap," I said.

Dane smiled at me and eased his hand between us to cup my tit. He circled the nipple with his thumb as the feeling of fullness increased.

"Oh," I moaned when Mason reached under me and palmed my pussy. He rubbed his fingers against my clit, and I squirmed against Dane as pleasure started to creep past the discomfort. "Oh, that feels good."

Mason was breathing hard and I could feel him sliding slowly in and out, each time sinking a little deeper into my ass. Finally, with a low groan, he stopped moving, his pelvis pressed against my ass, his hand still cupping my pussy.

"Okay?" he said.

"Fuck, I'm gonna cum," Dane said.

"Not you, jackass." Mason's voice was tight, and I giggled when Dane's cheeks turned red.

Both men groaned when I giggled, and I squeaked in surprise when they made two rough thrusts.

"Fuck!" Dane ground out as Mason's hands

moved to my hips and gripped hard. "Oh fuck, this might have been a bad idea."

The pain was completely gone now, and I was growing used to the feeling of being stuffed full of cock. In fact, I decided, I liked it a lot. A whole lot.

"It isn't," I said. "It feels really good. I like it."

"That's great, sweetheart." Mason's voice sounded weird and I craned my neck to look over my shoulder.

"Mason? Are you all right?" I moved experimentally and grinned when both men groaned again.

"Fuck, stop moving," Mason said. "Just for a goddamn minute, I am fucking begging you."

"You guys act like you've never double teamed a girl before," I said before rocking between them.

"Oh my God!" Dane's hands grabbed my waist and he made another three hard thrusts as Mason bellowed out a curse behind us.

Their reaction was like a damn drug to me. I'd never seen either of them lose control like this so quickly, and I was determined to tease and torment.

"Control, gentlemen," I said, then squeezed my pussy and my ass simultaneously.

They both cried out, and I laughed before kissing Dane's chest and propping myself up on my hands above him.

"Naomi, please," Dane moaned.

"Fuck me," I said. "Fuck me hard and fast. Both of you."

They didn't need to be told twice. I grabbed Dane's shoulders and held on as the two men thrust in and out in a smooth and practiced rhythm. My delight at their lack of control, my desire to tease them, had disappeared in a haze of pleasure so thick I was drowning it. The feel of their thick cocks in my body, the hard and heavy strokes as they drove in and out was sending waves of bliss throughout my body.

I strained for my pinnacle as both men moved faster. I knew I was on the knife edge of the best orgasm of my life. When Dane's hand slipped between us and his rough fingers rubbed my clit, I screamed and came so hard that bright stars of light flashed in my vision.

Vaguely I heard Mason bellow my name and hot wetness flooded my ass as his hands dug into my hips. Dane followed shortly after, moaning my name repeatedly as he thrust hard into my pussy. I collapsed against Dane, his heart a frantic staccato beat beneath my ear. Mason's forehead rested between my shoulder blades, his breath hot against my skin.

"Mason," Dane groaned, "move before you crush us."

Mason huffed out a breath before easing out of my ass and falling onto his side on the bed next to us. Dane kissed the top of my head and I kissed his chest before sliding off his body onto the mattress between them.

Dane ditched the condom and the three of us laid silently, our combined panting filling the bedroom. After about five minutes, I reached for both of their hands and squeezed them tight.

"Holy shit," Dane said. "That was incredible,

baby."

"Thank you," I said with a small grin. My eyes were still closed, and I squeezed Mason's hand when he didn't say anything. "You okay, honey? Was it a good birthday gift?"

"The fucking best birthday gift," Mason said. His voice sounded dazed and I cracked open one eye. He was staring at me, his gaze hazy with remembered pleasure. In a voice thick with satisfaction, he said, "Thank you for the birthday gift. I love you, sweetheart."

I froze, opening both eyes in a hurry as Dane sat up behind me. "What the fuck, Mason?"

Mason stared blankly at us, shaking his head as if to clear the fog. "What?"

"You just told her you fucking loved her!"

"I… what? No, I didn't."

"Yes, you goddamn did," Dane said.

For some reason, Dane looked flustered and worried. I stared up at him as he placed a staying hand on my hip. "Baby, don't panic."

I blinked at him. "I'm not panicking. I think you might be panicking."

"I'm fine!" Dane was almost shouting. "Just don't freak out or leave, okay? We can work through this."

"Work through what?" I said.

"The fact that we're both fucking in love with you, that's what!" Now he did shout, and Mason winced.

"Dane, just chill out."

Dane glared at him. "If she leaves, I'll never fucking forgive you, Mason. You told me not to say anything about being in love with her and then you just blurt it out!"

"I couldn't help it. I just had the best goddamn orgasm of my life," Mason said.

"So did I, but you didn't see me telling her how much I love her. Jesus Christ." Dane ran his hand through his hair. "I can't believe you did that. If she leaves…"

I sat up, the excitement coursing through my body giving way to confusion. "Why would I leave?"

"Because we love you," Dane said. "And Mason said it's too fucking early to tell you that, which I disagreed with by the way – I wanted to tell you immediately – but he said if we did, you'd freak out and leave. So I kept my goddamn mouth shut and then jackass over here just fucking says it and -"

"It was an accident!" Mason glared at Dane. "I didn't mean to tell her, but I was so happy and -"

"Like I'm not?" Dane said. "I've been walking on the fucking moon since she moved in with us, but I kept my damn feelings to myself for the last two months. You manage to keep it a secret for what… two hours? Is that when you realized you loved her too – two hours ago? Jesus, two fucking hours, Mason."

"It was a lot longer than that," Mason said. "I just didn't want to admit it, but I've loved her for as long as you have, Dane."

"It's not a competition. We both love her, end of story. Until you had to go and fuck it up because -"

"It was an accident," Mason said. "Holy fuck, I told you that. Look, I screwed up, but we'll just tell Naomi that it's okay that she doesn't love us and we're not trying to put any pressure on her."

"Like that's gonna fucking work," Dane said. "You were the one freaking out earlier about her leaving us, and now you're acting like -"

"If she leaves us, I'll fix it."

"How? How the fuck are you gonna fix it? You've blown it, Mason."

"Stop being so negative, Dane. Christ, I -"

"Negative? I'm not negative. I'm simply pointing out that -"

I put my hands over both of their mouths, stopping the flow of words and the argument. Before they could say anything, I said, "I love you too. Both of you."

I could feel their jaws dropping open behind my palms. I lowered my hands and said, "I've been in love with you for weeks now. Since you barged into my father's house and rescued me."

"You love us," Dane said.

"Why do you look so surprised?" I said. "I should be the one who's surprised you're in love with me. If we're being honest, I bring nothing to the relationship and I still can't believe that you guys love me."

"You are everything to us." Mason cupped my face and kissed me hard on the mouth. "We're lost without you."

Dane pressed up against me, turning my face so he could kiss me too. "He's right, baby. We love you and we're never giving you up.

Happiness was filling every molecule of my body. They loved me. Holy crap, they loved me.

"Never," Mason said. "Your ours forever, sweetheart."

"I like the sound of that," I said.

"We do too," Dane said.

I relaxed on my back, pulling both of my men down beside me. They curled into me, stroking my body with their warm hands as I smiled contently. They loved me. It wouldn't be easy having a relationship with both of them, but we'd make it work. I knew it without a doubt.

Chapter Fourteen

Dane

"What are you up to?" Naomi kissed my cheek before sitting on the stool next to me.

She sipped at her coffee. The early morning sunlight beamed in through the window and across the island to the far wall, lighting up her dark hair and making it shine even more than usual.

"Trying to find out some information," I said as Mason wandered into the kitchen.

It'd been over a week since we'd all confessed our love and it'd been the happiest time of my life. Spending time with Naomi and Mason, in and out of the bedroom, was exactly what I wanted, and I had no fucking idea how I'd gotten so lucky.

Still, there was something that I wanted to do for Naomi, and it was bugging the shit out of me that I couldn't do it.

"Information on what?" Naomi said.

I glanced at Mason. He knew what I was up to, I'd talked to him about it yesterday at work, but I wasn't sure that I wanted Naomi to know yet.

"You should tell her," Mason said.

"Tell me what?" Naomi asked.

I cleared my throat. "I'm trying to find the guy that your sister is with."

Naomi paused with her coffee cup halfway to her mouth. "Seriously?"

"Yeah. I've been doing some googling, but I think the name you told me is a fake one. The guy who keeps coming up is a lawyer from Connecticut."

Naomi set her cup down and wrapped her arms around me, hugging me hard before pressing a kiss against my lips. "I love you. Thank you for trying. Can I see the picture of the guy?"

I turned my laptop toward her, and she studied the guy on the screen before shaking her head. "It's not him."

"You've seen him?"

She nodded. "Yeah, he came to the house to get Joy."

"Jesus," Mason said. "I can't believe that your father just gave her to some fucking rando."

Naomi's face was pale, and she fidgeted on the stool. "I think about her every day and worry about her so much."

"I know, baby," I said. It was why I wanted to find her sister. I hated that Naomi wasn't completely happy.

I took a sip of my own coffee before closing my laptop. "I want to suggest something, and I'd like you to consider it. Don't just automatically say no, okay?"

"Okay," she said.

"Mason and I want to hire a private detective," I said.

"But if we don't even know the guy's real name, how will that help?" Naomi said.

"You'd be surprised what they can dig up," Mason said. "He'll talk to some of the other members in the cult your father belongs to, he may be able to get some true information from them. It's worth a shot, right?"

"How much will that cost?" Naomi said.

"It doesn't matter," I said. "We want to do this for you, baby. Let us."

To my shock, she nodded. "All right. Thank you."

Mason grunted in surprise and Naomi smiled wanly. "I love her, and I just want her back with me where she's safe."

"We'll do everything we can to make that happen," I said.

Naomi stared into her coffee cup. "I might be able to help."

"What do you mean?" Mason said.

"I'm having coffee with my mother in about half an hour. I could ask her about the guy. See if she knows his real name or has more information about where he's living. I know it's some sort of commune just outside of the city, but -"

"You're having coffee with your mother?" Mason's voice was hard.

"Yes," she said.

"No, you're not," I said.

Her face turned red and she slid from the stool.

"Don't, Dane."

"It's too dangerous," I said. "Naomi, you can't have coffee with her. It's probably a trap."

She snorted and turned to Mason. "Tell him how ridiculous he's being, please."

To my relief, Mason said, "He's right. Having coffee with your mother is a very bad idea, Naomi."

"I've already had coffee with her twice," Naomi said.

I pushed back my stool, anger and fear twisting through my veins. "You did what?"

She didn't flinch at my angry tone. "She was waiting for me outside the office one day last week when I left for lunch. I agreed to try and have a relationship with her again. She knows that I'm not interested in trying to mend things with my father and has agreed to make this about just us."

"Are you insane?" Mason rarely lost his cool, but now he was pacing the kitchen like an angry tiger. "She is using you, Naomi!"

"No, she isn't," Naomi said. "My mother misses me. Is that so hard to believe?"

"No," I said, "but your mom isn't a good mother. She let your father fucking sell you to another guy. Have you forgotten that?"

"Of course, I haven't," Naomi said. Her hands clenched into tight fists. "But she asked for my forgiveness and I gave it to her."

"Naomi, you're being naïve," Mason said. "She's getting close to you again because -"

"Because I'm her daughter and she loves and misses me, and because she's as much of a victim of my father as Joy and I are," Naomi said. "I know you want her to be this monster, but she isn't. You don't know her the way I do."

Before we could argue further, Naomi grabbed her purse from the counter and slipped it over her shoulder. "I'll be back in a little while. I'll ask my mother if she has any information on this guy, okay?"

"Please don't go," Mason said. "It's too dangerous."

"It isn't," she said. "We're in a public place and nothing is going to happen. I'll be fine."

"Let us go with you," I said. "We won't say anything or do anything but -"

"No," she said. "I'm having coffee with my mother alone, Dane."

I grunted in reply and Naomi stuffed her cell phone into her purse. "Everything will be fine. I love you both and I'll see you in a couple of hours."

"At least tell us which coffee shop you're going to," Mason said. "Please, sweetheart."

She sighed. "Fine. It's the Starbucks at the corner of Clawson and West."

She left the kitchen and Mason slumped against the island when the front door slammed. "Shit."

I was already grabbing my phone and stuffing my keys into my pocket.

"What are you doing?" Mason said.

"Going to the Starbucks. She shouldn't be alone with her."

I waited for Mason to tell me I was being ridiculous. Instead, he grabbed his phone and followed me out of the kitchen.

❧ ❦

Naomi

"I don't know anything about him. Your father didn't give me any details other than his name. I didn't know it was a fake name," my mother said.

The little flicker of hope died in my chest. On the drive over, I'd half convinced myself that my mother would know exactly who the guy was and where his commune was.

Maybe she does. Maybe she's lying to you.

I shoved that voice out of my head. If I was going to have any type of relationship with my mom, I had to trust that she was making an effort and being truthful with me. Constantly doubting her motivations wouldn't help us create any sort of new relationship. I either trusted her or I didn't.

"Can you ask Dad?" I said. "He might know his real name."

She stared into her coffee cup, clearly unsettled by my request. The Starbucks was packed with people – not surprising for a Sunday afternoon – and I leaned closer so I didn't have to raise my voice to be heard over the hum of conversations. "Mom, it's important."

She didn't reply and I placed my hand over hers and squeezed. "I know you're scared to ask him, but if it means we can get Joy back, it's worth the risk, right?"

"Right," she whispered.

"The worse he can do is refuse to give you any information."

"But he'll want to know why I'm asking, and I won't know what to say."

The whine in my mother's voice made me grit my teeth. She's a victim too, I reminded myself. It's not her fault that she's a scared little mouse.

"She's your daughter too," I said. "You have the right to know who she's with and how she's doing."

"Your father says she's fine."

I was starting to get a headache. "You can't trust that he's telling you the truth. There's no possible way she can be fine. She's being held against her will in a goddamn commune."

"Watch your language!" My mother's head snapped up, her cheeks a fiery red. "You know how your father hates it when women curse."

"I don't fucking care," I said deliberately.

My mother winced and part of me hated that I was upsetting her, but at the same time she needed to know that I'd no longer be held to any standard my father set.

"No one cares if a woman curses, Mom. Look, what matters is Joy. If we know where she is, if we even know the real name of the man who has her, I might be able to help her. We can save her. Don't you want... Mom? What's wrong?"

My mother was staring over my shoulder, her eyes wide. "What are they doing here?"

"Who?" I turned in my seat to see Dane and Mason staring guiltily at me from a table near the door. My heart thudding in my chest, I yanked my phone out of my purse and sent a text to Dane.

Are you kidding me right now, Dane Wilson?

He checked his phone, colour rising high in his cheeks as Mason read the message over his shoulder.

My phone dinged.

We just wanted to make sure you were safe.

I was so angry I could barely think straight. I shoved my phone into my purse and stood. "Mom, let's go."

"Go where?" She stared at me in bewilderment but stood up.

"Anywhere but here." I grabbed both of our coffees and marched toward the door, deliberately refusing to look at Dane and Mason as I passed by them.

దం ఆం

Naomi

I took a deep and calming breath before I opened the door and stepped inside. It was almost six hours later. After finishing coffee with my mother, I'd called Jemma and gone for dinner with her. Both Mason and Dane had texted me, and while I was tempted to be a total child and completely ignore their texts, I hadn't.

As much as they pissed me off by following me to the coffee shop, I still loved them both and I wouldn't deliberately worry them. I'd replied with a quick text letting them know that I had dinner plans and would be home later before turning my phone to mute and shoving it into my purse.

I kicked off my shoes and headed to the living room. Dane and Mason were sitting on the couch with mutual pissed off looks on their faces.

"Where have you been?" Dane said.

"I told you. I had dinner plans."

"With your mother?" Mason said.

"What does it matter who I had dinner with?"

Dane snorted like an angry bull and Mason glared at me. "It matters because we can't keep you safe if we have no fucking idea where you are or who you're with."

"I appreciate that you want to keep me safe," I tried to keep my voice calm even though I was a little pissed off myself, "but you also need to trust me when I say I'm not in any danger."

"Please," Dane's voice practically dripped with sarcasm, "you have no idea how dangerous it is out there. You've lived your entire life in a goddamn bubble, Naomi."

"I'm aware of that, but I'm also not stupid," I said.

"You need to let us know in the future who you're having dinner with," Mason said. "This isn't negotiable."

Red hot fire seared my veins. "You did not just say that, Mason."

He flushed but crossed his arms over his chest. "Yes, I did. Dane and I spoke while you were gone and we both agree that until you understand a little more how the world works, and how much danger your family poses to you, you need to let us accompany you to anything you do with your mother."

"Is that right," I said.

"Yes." Dane mimicked Mason and crossed his

arms over his chest. "It's for your safety, baby."

"Look, I love you both for wanting to take care of me and keep me safe, but you promised me you wouldn't try and control me. I am more than happy to do what you say in the bedroom, but outside of it, I do what I want."

"You're deliberately putting yourself in danger!" Dane said.

"I'm not. My mother isn't a monster," I said.

"She sold you to a perverted old man!" Mason shouted.

I jammed my fists on my hips. "And I told you I've forgiven her for that. Look, it's not just that she's my mom. She's also my only chance of getting my sister back, okay? I don't want to destroy this relationship if it means I have any chance of saving Joy. Why can't you understand that?"

"We do understand," Dane said. "We want you to get Joy back. All we're asking is that you talk to us first about visiting with your mother. If we think it's a good idea, then you can visit her while we're with you and -"

"If you think it's a good idea," I repeated.

Dane flushed. "If we think it's *safe*, then we'll let you -"

"You need to stop right there," I said. "Before you say something that you can't walk back."

"Naomi, you need -"

"No." I glared at Mason. "You be quiet as well, please."

I took two deep breaths. "I am not a child and while I appreciate everything you have done and are doing for me, I won't be controlled. Not anymore."

"That's not what we're doing," Mason said.

"It is," I said. "We all know it."

"There's a difference between trying to control you and caring for you," Dane said. "It's not our fault you can't see that difference. We don't want to tell you what to do, we just want -"

"To tell me what to do when it comes to my mother. That is the very definition of controlling, Dane. If the two of you can't see that, then I'm not sure that a relationship is the best thing for any of us."

Dane's face paled and so did Mason's. I hated that I was hurting them but at the same time, anger still flowed through my veins like thick and fiery lava. Their inability to admit that they were trying to control me, hurt me to my core. I wanted – *needed* – them to be different from my father.

We stared silently at each other for close to a minute before I took a step back. "I'm going to sleep in my own room tonight. I need some space."

"We love you," Dane said. "Naomi, try to see it from our point of view. If something were to happen to you…"

"I love you too," I said. "But I need space and time to figure out what's best for us. I won't be controlled ever again and right now, I'm not sure that you two truly understand that."

Chapter Fifteen

Naomi

"Seriously, you look like your best friend has died," Jemma said as we headed back to the office. "Please tell me what's wrong."

"It's nothing," I said. "I'm just tired and feeling emotional."

"Are you sure?" Jemma took my arm before I could open the lobby door of our office building. "I thought maybe taking you for lunch would cheer you up, but you don't look any happier, honey."

I smiled at her. "Thank you for lunch by the way. It was really lovely of you."

"Hey, it's what friends do. Besides, it was Taco Tuesday at Alberto's, and you know how I love my tacos."

"They are pretty good," I said.

Jemma was still holding my arm and she gave it a squeeze. "You know if there's something you want to talk about, I'm a pretty good listener."

"I know," I said. "It's complicated."

"I get it," she said.

She didn't, but that wasn't her fault. I couldn't exactly tell her that I was in love with two men but for the last two days I'd been basically avoiding both of them because I didn't know what the hell to do. Avoiding them at home and at work took herculean effort, especially since I sat right outside Dane's damn office, but I was making it happen.

I needed to. I was still angry and upset that they were trying to control me after promising they wouldn't, and I hadn't gotten any closer to figuring out if I could trust that this was a one time thing or if it was setting a precedent for our relationship.

They made a mistake, Naomi. Give them the chance to prove to you they won't do it again.

I wanted to, but I needed to be very careful. They were right in that I was on the naïve side and I didn't know much about the outside world. But maybe Dane and Mason didn't have my best interests at heart, despite loving me.

They do. For God's sake, they are nothing like your father and if you would just look at this logically for a damn second, you'd see that they deserve a second chance.

They liked control though, that was obvious, and they could tell me all they wanted that they were only looking for it in the bedroom, but their reactions and what they'd said on Sunday proved otherwise.

"Naomi?" Jemma was shaking my arm gently. "Your phone is buzzing."

I stared blankly at her before grabbing my phone out of my purse. I stared at the text message and accompanying picture, my mouth dropping open as hope and confusion soared through me at once.

"What's wrong?" Jemma looked over my shoulder. "She's pretty. Who is that?"

"My sister," I said.

"I didn't know you have a sister."

"I have to go," I said. "Can you do me a favour and tell Dane that I had a personal emergency and I need to take the afternoon off."

"Uh, okay," Jemma said. "Is everything all right?"

"I think it might be," I said as a smile spread across my face. "I have to go."

I turned and sprinted for my car in the parking lot.

❧ ❦

Mason

"We fucked up."

"You think I don't fucking know that?" Dane paced back and forth in his office. "I know, Mason. I goddamn know."

"She hasn't said a word to me since Sunday. I miss her."

"I miss her too," Dane said.

"You get to at least talk to her at work." I sounded like a sulky little kid and Dane glared impatiently at me.

"Only work-related stuff and, believe me, she keeps it as short as possible. She barely looks at me."

"What are we going to do?" I said.

"Give her more time and space."

I slammed my fist down on Dane's desk. "I can't do this for much longer."

"Too fucking bad. We have to prepare ourselves that she may never forgive us. Like you said – we fucked up."

"What were we thinking?" I wanted to smash my fist into Dane's desk again but resisted.

"We weren't. We let our emotions get the best of us. I didn't mean to try and control her, and I know you didn't either, but that's exactly what we did. And refusing to admit it, trying to conceal it as some kind of fucked up way of caring for her, was the exact wrong fucking thing to do."

"I'll go crazy if she leaves us," I said.

Dane stared grimly at me. "If it comes to that, if she says she's leaving, the two of us will get down on our fucking knees and beg her to stay."

"Goddamn right we will," I said.

There was a knock on his office door and Dane said, "Come in."

"Mr. Wilson?" Jemma poked her head into the office. "I just got back from lunch with Naomi, and she asked me to tell you that she had a personal emergency and she needed to take the rest of the day off."

Dane's big body stiffened. "What? Where is she?"

"Oh, um, I don't know," Jemma said. "She just got a text and then she -"

"Who was the text from?" I could hear the anxiety in my voice and evidently Jemma could too because she stared curiously at me.

"She didn't say."

"She didn't say," Dane repeated. He looked at me and I could see my anxiety reflected in his face.

"What's going on?" Jemma said slowly. "Why are you both acting so freaked out?"

"We're fine," Dane said. "We're just worried about her. A personal emergency doesn't sound good."

"Well, I'm sure it isn't anything bad," Jemma said. "She seemed kind of happy when she got the picture."

"What picture?" I said.

"Of her sister."

My stomach dropped and my anxiety turned to full-blown panic. Dane was already reaching for his phone and he smiled distractedly at Jemma. "Thanks for letting us know. Leave now."

Jemma blinked in surprise before closing the door. I turned to Dane, trying to keep the panic out of my voice. "Her sister? What the fuck, Dane?"

He was checking his phone. "She hasn't texted me. Has she texted you?"

I grabbed my phone out of my pocket. "No."

"Fuck."

"I'm calling her," I said. I scrolled through my contacts and was about to press Naomi's number when Dane scooped my phone out of my hand.

I glared at him. "Give me my phone, asshole."

"We can't call her," he said.

"If it's something to do with her sister, then she's in danger," I said.

"We don't know that. Maybe Naomi's right.

Maybe her mother isn't the monster we think she is and has somehow gotten her sister back."

"You don't really believe that," I said.

"I don't know what to believe." Dane's mouth was a hard slash. "But I do know if we call her or chase after her, we will fucking lose her, Mason."

"But -"

"We will," he said. "We're close to losing her now."

All the air oozed out of me and I sat on the corner of his desk, my head in my hands. "I fucking hate this. Something doesn't feel right."

"I know," Dane said. "But we have to trust that Naomi knows what she's doing and that if she needs us, she'll call us."

"What if she doesn't call?" I said hoarsely. "What if we really have lost her?"

"We just have to hope like fucking hell that we haven't, Mason."

Naomi

I didn't bother knocking on the door of my parents' home. I threw open the door and barrelled in like an out of control train. I didn't give a second thought to whether my father would be there, I didn't care. All I cared about was Joy.

"Mom!" My voice was shrill with excitement. "Mom, where are you?"

I ran into the kitchen without waiting for her reply, skidding to a stop just beyond the doorway with my heart in my throat and tears already starting to leak down my face. "Joy?"

My sister ran toward me and I met her halfway, flinging my arms around her and hugging her so hard, she made a small groan of pain. "Joy, oh, honey. I can't believe you're here."

Laughing and crying, I cupped her face and stared at her. "Are you okay?"

She nodded. "I'm okay, Naomi. Really glad to see you."

"Me too." I stepped back and looked her over. She was wearing a long skirt, her shirt was buttoned to her throat, and her dark hair was covered by a scarf. Her face was make-up free and there were a few more small lines around her eyes and mouth, but otherwise she looked the same.

"You look good," I said.

She half-shrugged before studying me. "You look better."

"How did this happen?" I said.

Joy stared at our mother who was leaning against the counter. "I don't know. This morning Robert told me I was free to go, and he had two of his," she grimaced, "followers drive me here."

"Mom," I said, "did you do this? Did you convince Dad to bring Joy home?"

My mother swallowed hard. Weirdly, she didn't seem happy or relieved. She was pale and she was biting compulsively at the hangnails on her fingers, a sure sign of her anxiety.

"Mom," I said, "how did you make this happen?"

"She didn't. I did."

I whirled, automatically tucking Joy behind me

as I stared with loathing at Deacon Dennison.

"Get out," I said. "Get out of my house, right now."

"It's not your house," he said with a roll of his eyes. "And you should be thanking me, Naomi. I brought your precious sister home."

"What's he talking about?" Joy said.

"Hello, Joy. It's good to see you again," Dennison said. "You're looking well. Was your time with Robert a productive one?"

"Don't talk to her!" I spat at him. "Don't talk to her and don't look at her."

"Do you think because you're wearing whore clothing and whore makeup, you can speak to me in that tone?" he said. "Because I can assure you, when we're married, you'll learn quickly what happens when you're disrespectful."

I barked jagged laughter. "I'm not marrying you, asshole. I don't care what my father said or promised you, I'm not -"

"Oh, it wasn't your father," Dennison said.

I could feel the blood draining from my face. I stared at my mother. "Where's Dad?"

Dennison laughed. "The last I heard, he was at the casino, spending his paycheques and leaving your poor mother destitute and almost homeless. That money your heathen friends gave him didn't last very long, did it, Alice? Not with his gambling habit. Luckily, I'm here to bail you out, again."

"Mom," I whispered, "what have you done?"

"I had no choice," she said. "Naomi, we're behind on paying everything, including the mortgage. We're going to lose the house."

"So, you sold me, just like Dad did?" Hurt roared through me and my throat closed up to a pinhole. I dragged in a whistling breath. "You're my mother. How could you?"

"Sold is such a nasty word," Dennison said. "It's really more of a negotiation. Isn't that right, Alice?"

"I don't care how much money you give her," I said. "I'm not going with you. She and my father can live on the goddamn streets for all I fucking care."

"Such a filthy mouth." Dennison's brow furrowed into a scowl. "What did those wretched beasts of men teach you?"

"Cursing isn't all they taught me," I said. "I'm not your sweet little virgin anymore, asshole."

His face went red and his hands clenched into fists. "You little slut. You couldn't wait to give it away, could you?"

I just grinned at him, but the grin faded when he shrugged and said, "It doesn't matter. I'll make sure you're cleansed before I lay with you."

"I'm not letting you touch me," I said.

"Of course, you are," he said. "I'll be your husband and it's the wife's duty to lay with her husband."

"Fuck you!" I was terrified but doing my best to hide it behind a mask of scorn and anger. "I'm not going anywhere with you. In fact, you have ten seconds to get out of this house before I call the cops."

"Call them and you'll never see your sister again."

I automatically clutched Joy a little closer to me. "Just try and take her from me, asshole."

He chuckled and fear tingled down my spine when he said, "I don't have to do it. The men who brought her here will do it for me."

He snapped his fingers and two men wearing dark suits walked into the kitchen. I backed away with Joy still tucked behind me, hot fear making my lungs seize up. The men weren't on the large side but there would be no way I could stop them if they tried to take Joy from me.

"These gentlemen will be more that happy to return Joy to her husband," Dennison said.

"He's not my husband," Joy said.

Dennison waved his hand in the air. "You belong to him, little girl." He leveled a cold look at me. "Here's the deal your mother has made, Naomi. She gets her bills paid and keeps a roof over her head, and her beloved first daughter is returned to her. I get her ungrateful little brat of a youngest. You don't come with me, the deal ends. Your mother ends up on the street doing who knows what to survive, and Joy is returned to her rightful owner."

His gaze flickered to Joy. "You know, I had a hard time convincing Robert to give you up. He said he was just getting ready to bless you with child."

Joy stiffened behind me and I heard her sharp intake of breath. I glanced up at her, adrenaline pumping through my veins at the look of fear on her face.

"Well, what will it be, Naomi? Will you honour

your mother's deal, or will you watch your sister be returned to her husband while you continue with your whoring ways?"

I took a deep breath as a merry-go-round of wild ideas ricocheted through my head ranging from grabbing a knife and trying to stab the three men to bursting into tears and begging Dennison to let all of us go.

I grimaced inwardly, none of them were even remotely helpful.

Dane and Mason. You need them.

Some of the fear running through me, eased off a little. Mason and Dane would save me.

Really? You've barely spoken to them the last two days. You've been ignoring them like a pouty little kid. Why would they care what happens to you?

I ignored that new voice in my head. Dane and Mason loved me. That hadn't changed just because we argued.

"Naomi?" Dennison's voice was hard. "What will it be?"

"I'll go with you," I said.

"Like hell you will," Joy said. She tried to pull away from me and I clung to her, shaking my head.

"It's fine, Joy."

"No, it isn't! You're not going with him. I'll go back to Robert. I'm not ruining your life or -"

"Joy." I cupped her face and stared directly at her. "It's fine. I want to do this. You deserve to be free. I *want* to do this."

I stared intently at her, praying inwardly that we hadn't been apart for so long that she could no longer understand my silent communication. She searched my face before slowly nodding. "All right."

I turned to face Dennison. "I'll go with you, but I need to call Mason and Dane first."

"No," he said.

"I have to. If I don't tell them that I'm quitting my job and that I'm moving out of their home, they won't stop searching for me. They're in love with me and they have the money and the power to find me if they think I've been taken against my will. I'll call them and tell them it's over between us."

"Bullshit," Dennison said. "You're lying to me."

"I'm not," I insisted. "You've seen them. Do you really want them going after you?"

His face paled and I cheered inwardly. My plan depended on him being a coward and apparently my instincts about him were right.

"Call him," he said. "But you do it right here and if you say anything to them about what's happening, these two men will take your sister and you'll never see her again. You understand?"

"I understand," I said.

Trying to keep my hands from shaking, I pulled out my cell and called Dane. He answered on the first ring and I almost burst into tears.

"Baby? Where are you?"

I held the phone tight to my ear, so the others couldn't hear his voice. "Hello, Dane."

"You okay?"

"I'm fine," I said.

"Jemma said something about your sister."

Dane's voice soothed me even if he sounded confused and a little anxious.

"Yes, she's back home.   Listen, I have something I need to say. It's over between us."

There was a long drawn out silence and I held my breath, my temples throbbing with the heavy beat of my pulse.

"No," Dane said.

I could have wept with relief at the familiar stubbornness in his voice. I could hear the muffled sound of Mason's voice and Dane said, "She wants to end things with us."

"It's over," I said again.

"Baby, no," Dane said. "I know you're upset and yes, Mason and I crossed the line with what we said and did, but I swear we understand how fucked up it was, and we won't do it again. We're begging you to give us -"

"No," I said loudly. "It's over. Things have been bad between us for the last three weeks and I'm over it. I never wanted this to be a long-term thing. You were just an experiment for me. If I thought it was serious, don't you think I would have said I love you by now?"

Please Dane, please understand.

There was another long pause and then Dane said, "Baby, is your dad with you? Is he making you say these things?"

Now I did have to blink back the tears. "Yes. It's true."

"Are you at your parents' place? Do you want us to come and get you?" Dane said.

"Yes, that's exactly what I want," I said. I

paused and added, "No, I'm not going to change my mind. It's over between us."

"We're on our way, baby. Hold tight," Dane said.

Dennison made a motion for me to hang up the phone and I said, "Goodbye, Dane. Don't try and contact me again."

I ended the call, and Dennison grunted in satisfaction. Suddenly furious, I turned to my mother. "You're as much of a monster as Dad."

My mother gasped. "Naomi, please. I'm doing this for your own good. Being with two men – it's, it's an abomination. You'll go to hell. I'm saving you and your sister."

"No," I said, "you're saving yourself. You don't give a fuck about Joy or me."

"That's enough, Naomi," Dennison said. "Your foul language will no longer be tolerated. Let's go."

Icy panic gripped me again. "What? Go where?"

"To my home, of course," Dennison said.

I clutched Joy's hand. It would take Mason and Dane at least fifteen minutes to get here if they left immediately and the traffic wasn't bad. I needed to stall. "Can I have some time with my sister before we go?"

"No," Dennison said impatiently. "I have things to do, Naomi. Come." He held out his hand and I took a step back.

"Half an hour is all I'm asking for. I haven't seen her in years."

"You'll see her at church on Sunday and, if you

behave and do as I say, I'll allow her to visit you at our home from time to time. Now, let's go."

"Please," I said.

He huffed out an impatient laugh. "Are you going to be this way always, Naomi? Will I be required to bring you to heel on a daily basis? You will do as I say without argument or I will have these men take your sister and leave right now. We leave now or the deal is over."

I hugged Joy hard and whispered in her ear, "It'll be okay. They'll find me."

She was starting to cry, and I wiped at the tears roughly. "Don't cry, Joy. I love you."

"I love you too, Naomi," she said.

"Naomi," my mother said, "I love you, honey."

I looked her square in the face. "I hate you. I hope you burn in hell for what you've done."

She staggered back, her hand fluttering up to her mouth as she stared at me like a wounded bird. I didn't care. I meant every word I said.

Chapter Sixteen

Dane

"Do we call the police or not?" Mason said as I drove toward Naomi's parents' place.

"Not yet," I said.

"If he keeps trying to kidnap her, we can't just let that fucking go," Mason said.

"We don't know that he's kidnapped her," I said.

"She called us and asked us to come get her. If she can't leave on her own, then it's a fucking kidnapping and we should call the police," Mason said. "What if we get there and he has a goddamn gun?"

"Look, Naomi sounded nervous but not terrified," I said. "If her old man had a gun on her, she would have sounded more afraid."

"You better hope you're right," Mason said.

"Fuck, is her parents place on Thompson Boulevard or Crescent?" I slammed my hand down on the steering wheel. "I don't fucking remember."

"Crescent," Mason said. "Turn left here. Her parents' place is the blue bungalow with the white picket fence."

I silently thanked God for Mason's memory as I drove down the street.

"There's Naomi's car. Thank Christ," Mason said.

I parked on the street behind Naomi's car and both Mason and I ran up to the house. I pounded on the front door. "Naomi! Naomi, open the door!"

I tried the door handle, rattling it uselessly when it was locked. "Naomi! Open the door!"

Mason glanced around the neighbourhood. "Dane, lower your voice a little. We don't need the whole neighbourhood out here."

"I don't fucking care," I said before pounding on the door for a third time. "Open this fucking door right now, you son of a bitch, or I'll fucking kick it in!"

I was just getting ready to try and bust my way in when the door opened, and Naomi's mother stared at us. "Go away. Naomi isn't here and I'll call the police if you don't leave."

I pushed my way past her, Mason on my heels, and strode down the hallway. "Naomi! Baby, where are you?"

I ducked into the living room. It was empty and I followed Mason down the hall to the kitchen.

"Sweetheart?" Mason stepped into the kitchen. "Naomi, are you in here? Fuck!"

Naomi's mother had followed us in, and she stood near the doorway, holding her cell phone in her hand. "I told you she wasn't here. Leave. She broke up with you and doesn't want to see you anymore."

"Like fuck she did," I snarled. "Where did your husband take her?"

She didn't answer and I took a step toward her, my skin tight and my body tingling with panic. "Where the fuck is he? Answer me!"

"It wasn't Dad."

Mason and I stared at the woman who stepped into the kitchen. She was dressed much like Naomi used to dress with a scarf that covered her hair. I'd never seen a picture of Naomi's sister, but I knew she was Joy.

"Where is she, Joy?" I said.

"Deacon Dennison left with her about five minutes ago," she said. "My mother made a deal with him. He paid off her debts and brought me home, and she would give him Naomi."

"Are you fucking kidding me," Mason said.

"I had no choice," Naomi's mother said. "Josiah gambled away all the money you gave us. We're going to be homeless and… and you two were corrupting my baby girl!"

"You fucking sold your baby girl to a perverted old man!" I shouted.

Mason gripped me by the arm. "Take a deep breath, Dane."

Joy swallowed hard. "I tried to stop her. I told her that I would go back to Robert. I didn't want her to do this, but she said she wanted to. She said everything would be fine and that you would find her."

"Damn fucking right, we will," I said.

I glared at Naomi's mother. "Where's this asshole deacon live?"

Her mouth pressed into a straight line and she shook her head defiantly. "I won't tell you. Naomi is better off with him."

"Lady, you are fucking delusional," Mason said. "You need to be in a goddamn nuthouse."

"Where does he live?" I repeated.

She shook her head again and I wanted to scream in frustration.

"Mom," Joy stood in front of her mother, "tell them where she is."

"I won't," her mother said. "Joy, you have to understand. I love you and I love Naomi, and I only -"

I flinched and Mason made a grunt of surprise when Joy slapped her mother across the face. Her mother cried out, grabbing at her cheek and staring in shock at Joy as she said, "Tell them where she is. Right now."

"I won't! You can't – ouch!"

Joy had slapped her again, this one was so hard, I could see the imprint of Joy's hand on her cheek. "Tell them, Mother. Tell them or I swear to fucking God, I will walk out this door and go straight to the police. I'll tell them that my own parents sold me into a cult. I'll expose Robert and his cult, and you and Daddy and Deacon Dennison will go to prison for the rest of your lives. So, I will give you one last fucking chance to tell them where he lives."

Her mother swallowed hard, her hand still pressed against her cheek. Her gaze flickered between mine and Joy's before she whispered,

"Rondeau Street. 785 Rondeau Street."

Mason pushed past me and held out his hand to Joy. "Let's go get your sister, Joy."

"Joy?" Her mother whispered when Joy took Mason's hand. "Don't leave me."

"Goodbye, Mother," Joy said, and followed Mason and I out of the kitchen without looking back.

ॐ ॐ

Naomi

"Sit down, Naomi." Dennison pointed to a kitchen chair.

I sank into it, folding my arms nervously across my torso as Dennison sank into the chair across from me. His smug self-satisfied smile made me want to punch him in the face. Instead, I tried to concentrate on how he would look when Dane and Mason came busting in and saved me.

How exactly are they going to do that, Naomi? They have no idea where he lives.

I tried not to let my inner voice panic me. They could google him if they had to, right? How hard was it in this day and age to find a person's address? Not that fucking hard.

"We should go over the duties I expect of you as my wife." Dennison tapped his fingers on the table. "You will be expected to clean and cook, as well as pleasing me in the bedroom."

My stomach twisted and he must have seen the disgust on my face because he said, "I can assure you, Naomi, that I am more than adept at pleasing a

238

woman in the bedroom."

"Oh yeah? Then why did your wife leave you?" I said.

His face reddened. "That's none of your business. You'll want to keep your smart mouth to yourself, Naomi. Your parents may have been lenient with you, but you'll find that I'm not nearly as willing to accept your attitude."

"Well, that's a shame, because my attitude is here to stay."

His smile was chilling. "You say that now. It'll change."

"Fuck you," I said.

He laughed. "Not until we're married, dear. And not until you've been cleansed of the stench of the two men you whored yourself out to."

He straightened in his chair and pulled his phone out of his pocket. "Tomorrow morning, two women from the church will be stopping by to perform the cleansing. You are expected to submit to it and not argue or complain over anything they do to you. Some of it will be... unpleasant, but you can think of it as your punishment for allowing those men to defile your innocence."

Was that a car door? I strained to hear over the tapping as Dennison texted on his phone.

"I know it's early, but why don't you get started on supper. I prefer an early dinner as it gives us more time for prayer and devotions before bed. You'll find meat in the freezer and produce in the fridge. Don't use too much salt, I have high blood pressure." Dennison stared at me over his phone. "Hop to it, Naomi."

Gritting my teeth, I stood and walked to the fridge. Deacon Dennison was about to be served a meal so fucking full of salt, he'd choke on it.

The knock on the door made us both pause. Dennison stared suspiciously at me. "Who is that?"

"How would I know?" I said as hope bloomed bright in my belly. "I'll find out."

"Stay right where you are," he barked before leaving the kitchen.

I waited a few seconds and then followed him, walking lightly and holding my breath. He stood at the front door. "Who is it?"

"Deacon Dennison? It's Joy. Can I speak to my sister please?"

"How did you get here?" Dennison said.

"Please, I must speak to her. I promise it won't take long."

Dennison unlocked the door and opened it. "How did you get here, Joy? You can't just -"

His squeal of fear when Dane stepped in front of Joy and grabbed him by his shirt collar made hysterical laughter bust out of my chest. Dane propelled him back into the house and slammed him up against the wall. "Where is she, you bastard? Where's Naomi?"

"Dane, she's there!" Mason was already shoving past Dane. I started to cry when he ran to me and threw his arms around me.

He hugged me hard as Dane joined us. Both of them kissed my face repeatedly and I flung my arms around them and buried my face in Dane's chest.

"It's okay, baby. We have you now," he said.

"I love you," I said. "I'm sorry I was angry

with you. I love you both so much."

"We love you too," Mason said. "And we deserved your anger."

"You didn't." More tears spilled down my cheeks and Dane wiped them away with his thumbs.

"Don't cry, baby. You're safe now."

"Get out of my house," Dennison's voice was an anxious squeak.

Dane turned and glared at him. "Shut the fuck up before I knock your teeth down your throat."

Dennison shrank back against the wall as Joy joined us. I squirmed free of Mason and Dane's embrace and hugged her. "Hi, honey."

She kissed my forehead. "Are you okay?"

"Yeah. You?"

"Never better." She managed a small smile before glancing at the two men standing protectively behind me. "Your guys seem nice."

I laughed. "They're amazing."

"You're amazing." Dane kissed the top of my head. "C'mon, baby, let's get the fuck out of here."

Holding Joy's hand tightly, I headed toward the door, not even bothering to look in Dennison's direction. Mason slammed the door shut behind us and when Joy stopped, I squeezed her hand and smiled at her.

"We're free," she said with soft wonderment in her voice.

"Yes." I turned to smile at Mason and Dane, my love for them overwhelming in its intensity. "Let's go home."

Epilogue

One year later

Naomi

"Fuck, I'm glad that's over." Mason sank down on the couch with a groan, loosening his tie with one hand while Dane poured three glasses of whiskey. I slipped out of my heels and sat next to Mason, tucking my legs up under me and smoothing down my dress as Dane handed a glass of whiskey to Mason.

"Thank you for going today. It meant a lot to me and to Joy." I took the glass of whiskey from Dane and rested my free hand on his thigh when he sat down on the other side of me.

"Of course," Dane said. "We wouldn't have missed the sentencing, it's the best part."

I laughed and leaned my head on Mason's shoulder. "It was rather satisfying to see the look on Dennison's face when he got fifteen years in prison for human trafficking."

Dane's big hand massaged my thigh. "I know the last year has been hard for both you and Joy. Do you think she regrets going to the police about the cult and about Dennison?"

"No," I said. "It's been difficult, but she couldn't leave the other women in Robert's cult. She needed to save them too."

"And she did," Mason said.

"She did." A smile crossed my face. "Did I tell you that she and Meredith found a place?"

"Oh yeah?" Dane said.

"Yes. Money will be a little tight because they're both in University, but they found part time jobs and Joy said they'll make it work. She was closest to Meredith during her exile in the cult and I know she's glad they're living together."

"What about the other women?" Mason said.

I shrugged. "I'm not exactly sure what everyone is doing now that the trial is over, and Robert is in prison for the rest of his life. They were all at his sentencing last week, but I didn't get a chance to talk to many of them."

I lapsed into silence and stared at the whiskey in my glass. The last year had been difficult but Joy going to the police and exposing Robert and his cult and sharing the information that Dennison supplied most of the women to Robert, had been the right thing to do. All of us were asked to testify at Robert and Dennison's trials, and I'd never loved Dane and Mason more than when they'd stepped up and testified without any hesitation.

"Thank you for everything you've done the last year," I said to my two men. "Letting Joy live with us for so long, testifying, paying for therapy for both of us… we can never repay you."

"You don't have to," Mason said. "It's a gift. One we were happy to give."

"Have you spoken with your parents?" Dane asked.

I took a sip of whiskey, letting it burn its way down my throat. "No. I told you – I'm never speaking to either of them again. I don't care what my therapist says. Besides, no one knows where my dad is anyway. Joy talked to my aunt last week, Mom is still living with her in Ohio, but she hasn't heard anything from Dad since the bank foreclosed on the house."

Mason kissed my head. "Sorry, sweetheart."

"I'm not," I said. "They deserve every bad thing that happens to them."

There was more silence before I smiled at them. "Enough talk about my parents and the trial. That's all in our past now and I want to concentrate on our future."

"I'll toast to that," Dane said.

He raised his glass and the three of us clinked glasses. "To our future," Dane said.

"Our future," Mason and I echoed.

The three of us drank and I smiled at them. "Now, what do you say we go upstairs to the bedroom."

"Don't you have studying to do?" Mason said. "Your exam is tomorrow night."

"I've been studying all week. It helps that Dane keeps giving me, like, two hours of study time at work every day."

Dane kissed my cheek. "I want you to do well, baby. Besides, you're so efficient at your job, it leaves plenty of free time in your day. You should be using that to study."

"Did I tell you that Jemma's mom asked me to redesign her kitchen?" I said.

"What? That's great!" Mason said.

"I know, right?" I couldn't stop my grin. "She didn't even care that I didn't have my design degree yet. Jemma showed her the photos of what I did to our kitchen and to the spare bedroom and her mom immediately hired me. I'm meeting with her next week to go over ideas."

"I'm so proud of you, baby," Dane said before kissing me. "We both are."

"Damn straight." Mason pressed a kiss against my mouth as well.

Familiar heat pooled in my belly and I smiled wickedly first at Dane and then at Mason. "Why don't you take me upstairs to the bedroom and show me exactly how proud you are of me with a pussy eating and then fucking?"

Both Mason and Dane laughed before draining their glasses and standing.

"Baby," Dane said as he helped me to my feet, "your wish is our command."

END

Please enjoy a sample chapter of Ramona Gray's novel "Sharing Del"

SHARING DEL

I'm twenty-five years old and I'm not a nice girl. Even my mama says I'm not nice. When I was sixteen, she sat me down and told me I was going to Hell. Told me that if I didn't see the light and walk the straight and narrow, God would strike me down with every bit of righteous vengeance he possessed.

At the time, I just chalked it up to her being mad. She had after all, just caught me sucking Tommy Robertson's cock in the confessional booth at our church. I can't help it. I like boys. I like them a lot. I'm not really into what you would call the monogamous relationships. I've tried. I swear to the Mother Mary I've tried, but after a few weeks or a few months I get bored and I'm moving on to my next conquest.

I tried girls for a while. Figured maybe my problem wasn't committing to one person but committing to one man. I hooked up with a bad girl named Raquel in my first year of college. Oh my sweet blazing Jesus, could that bitch eat pussy. I mean, the girl's tongue was *magic*.

Turns out though, my issue wasn't with men. After only a few months I was starting to get bored. I would have left Raquel if she hadn't left me first. Well, maybe her leaving me isn't exactly right. I packed my stuff and left when I came home one night and found her tongue-deep in the pussy of her lab partner. She called me a few times begging for forgiveness and I told her it was fine. I didn't tell her I was about to leave her anyway.

Even though she cheated on me, I didn't want to hurt her feelings and I'm kind of worried you know? Worried that there's something wrong with me that I can't commit to just one person. I have three older sisters and all of them are happily married to good Catholic boys and popping out babies like they alone are responsible for keeping the Earth's population going.

Last weekend I visited my oldest sister Angela. I left the city and headed for the suburbs, saying a silent prayer every few miles that my rust bucket of a car would make it. I sat at the dinner table, two toddlers clinging to my legs and a baby throwing up on my shirt and listened as Angela lectured me.

"Del, you're going to kill Mama and Daddy. You know that, right? They worry about you constantly. Mama spends all her time at Mass praying for your eternal soul. You need to find the right person, settle down and have babies. Children complete your life – trust me on this."

I rolled my eyes and wiped at the spit-up on my shirt. "Yeah, this feels like a really great time."

Angela frowned and took the baby, cooing softly to him before wiping his face clean with the hem of her shirt. "I mean it, Del. Daddy's been having anxiety attacks and Mama hardly sleeps at night. At least come to church with us once a month."

Good old Catholic guilt. It's alive and well in

my family. My parents have seven children and I'm smack dab in the middle and the only one they fret about. My baby brother Mitchell gave them some trouble for a few months in high school, but they straightened him out pretty quick. I'm the only one they never could figure out or fix. The fate of my eternal soul causes them a lot of heartache.

Of course, my eternal soul is the last thing I need to be worrying about right now. Paying my rent, eating more than one meal a day – now those are the things that I really needed to concentrate on.

I moved to the city on a whim. I was tired of living in my parent's basement in the suburbs. I was tired of listening to the lectures about why I failed at college and failed at relationships. Hell, why I failed at life.

I work at a dive bar on 17th Avenue. My tiny apartment on 5th Street has walls so thin you can hear my neighbour Jerry whacking off every night to reruns of the goddamn Golden Girls. My job and shitty apartment weren't in the best areas in the city, but I carried my mace and know how to use it.

The problem is that I was barely scraping by to begin with and now my landlord has decided to raise the rent. Nine hundred bucks a month for a shit-ass apartment so tiny I can barely turn around in it without banging into the walls. Nine hundred bucks so I can take a two-minute shower before the water turns cold. Nine hundred bucks to watch mold growing on the walls and get to listen to an old balding man named Jerry cry out Bea fucking Arthur's name in orgasmic pleasure every goddamn night.

I wasn't going to miss it. Well… maybe Jerry.

I had two weeks left before I needed to move, and I hadn't found anything in my budget. It left me with two choices – take a second job or get a new apartment with a roommate. I chose a second job because honestly? I don't play well with others. Except I hadn't found anything yet and time was rapidly running out.

"Del! You thinking of working tonight or ya just gonna stand there diddlin' yourself?"

I scowled at the bartender. Mark could be a real asshole sometimes. The owner Bill wasn't around a lot and Mark liked to pretend that he ran the place. I adjusted my short skirt, picked up my tray of drinks, and crossed the crowded bar.

It was Saturday night and it was going to be busy. Once a month Bill brought in a local band to play named "Killjoy". They always brought in a huge crowd. Their lead singer Jesse had vocals of gold and filled out a pair of leather pants better than any man I knew. The first few months I seriously considered trying to get into those leather pants but after watching the groupies throw their panties on stage and flash their tits, I stopped even considering it.

Not that I don't have a kickass body. I might be short but I'm curvy in all the right spots with a set of tits on me that could make a grown man cry. I've got long dark hair, bright blue eyes and thanks to my mama's side of the family, milky-white skin. Maybe if I wasn't about to be homeless, I'd have thought harder about seducing Jesse.

I set down all the mugs of beer but one at a table

full of frat boys.

"Sweetheart, you get better looking every time you walk over here." The leader of the group grinned at me with perfect white teeth. He was cute in a frat boy bratty kind of way. I briefly considered taking him home and showing him the night of his life and then rejected it. Fucking some random guy was no way to avoid my problems. Besides, he was too pretty for me. I liked them big and rough. Still, it didn't mean I couldn't flirt my way into big tips.

"Why thank you, handsome," I purred and leaned over him, letting him get a good look down my shirt at my tits before I plucked the bills from his hand.

I turned to walk away and when he smacked me on the ass, I rolled my eyes before turning and giving him a wink. "You'd better watch it, big boy. You never know what I'll do with that hand."

"You can do anything you want to it, sweetheart." The frat boy grinned again as his friends laughed loudly.

I set the last beer down on the table in the corner farthest from the stage. "Hello, Cash."

"Del." The big man nodded and took a drink of beer before handing me a few bills. I counted out the change and held it out to him, but he shook his head. I nodded gratefully and shoved the bills into my apron pocket.

Cash came in once or twice a month and always sat in my section. He was quiet, kept his hands to himself and was a big tipper. My favourite kind of customer. I waited a moment to see if he would take a look at my tits, but his gaze had already shifted to the stage where the band was starting to set up.

I headed back toward the bar. Cash never looked at my tits, never made rude comments and never drank more than three beers. At first it kind of bugged me that he never made a pass, but after a while I found it refreshing. Not that I wouldn't have taken him up on it if he had. I mean, the man practically screamed sex and he was exactly the kind of man I liked. Big and broad shouldered, a permanent five o'clock shadow and tanned skin. Dark eyes and full lips, and if he didn't have a nice hairy chest that a girl could run her fingers through, I'd eat my own apron. He always wore a scuffed leather jacket with a tight t-shirt, jeans and worn cowboy boots. Once when I had snuck out back for a cigarette near the end of my shift, I had seen him leaving on a motorcycle, a big old Harley that roared loudly in the cool night air.

My pussy pulsed at the thought of riding behind Cash and my panties were suddenly wet. Christ, I really did need to get laid. I didn't have a chance with Cash, but the frat boy was starting to look better and better. There were sudden shrieks and I knew without looking that Jesse and the rest of Killjoy had taken the stage.

I leaned against the bar and watched for a few minutes. Jesse was wearing his usual leather pants only this time he had decided to go without the shirt. He usually ended up half-naked before the show was over anyway, guess he just decided it was pointless to even wear one. As he swayed in time to the music, I studied his upper torso. He was lean and absolutely ripped. Forget six pack, the man had a goddamn eight pack. His nipple rings glinted in the light and I thought about how nice it would be to pull on those rings with my teeth.

I shook my head. Jesus, I needed to get control of myself. My panties were soaked through and I was still leaking. I caught the eye of the frat boy and he gave me a wide grin. I smiled back. Frat boy wasn't my first choice, but he'd do.

→ ←

I slipped out the back door of the bar and studied the cigarette in my hand. I had quit six months ago, but occasionally bummed one from a co-worker. I lit the cigarette and inhaled deeply. The smoke hit my lungs in a soft rush, and I blew it out gently. God, it had been a long night and my feet were killing me.

I took another puff – I was already feeling a little dizzy from the nicotine – and leaned against the building. I had just finished cashing out and decided to have a quick smoke before I grabbed my things and took off. Frat boy and his friends had disappeared about ten minutes before the bar closed. I was disappointed but the part of me that wasn't a complete whore knew it was for the best. A night of fucking sounded good, but it wasn't going to solve my problems.

I sighed and took another drag on my cigarette. Tomorrow morning I'd –

"Hello, sweetheart."

I spun around. Frat boy was standing behind

me, leaning against the wall and smiling his straight-tooth grin at me.

"Well, hey there." I socked out my hip and lifted the cigarette to my lips. He watched me take a drag, watched the way my lips sucked at the thin white cylinder and his grin widened.

"Tell me, sweetheart, you got plans after work?"

I shrugged. "Depends."

"Depends on what?"

I stubbed out my cigarette and stepped closer. "Depends on you."

He kissed me, his tongue pushing into my mouth immediately. He had a large tongue and he was too eager and too determined to show me he was a good kisser. I pulled back and wiped my mouth off discreetly. Perhaps tonight wasn't going to be as fun as I thought.

"I've been wanting to kiss you all night." Frat boy grabbed my breast and squeezed it roughly.

"Slow down, handsome." I tugged his hand away. "Not so fast."

He pushed me up against the wall and cupped my breast again. "Please, you've been practically begging me for it all night."

I rolled my eyes, suddenly remembering why I didn't fuck college boys. "Give me a minute to -"

He kissed my neck, his teeth nipping at the skin and I pushed him away. "I said, slow down."

"Fine," he pouted and crossed his arms over his chest.

"Let me just grab my things and we'll go," I said.

He grinned and glanced behind his shoulder. I

followed his gaze, frowning when I saw his three buddies climbing out of the car.

"Do we get a group rate, sweetheart?"

Anger flooded through me and I spit on him. "I don't do groups, you little prick."

He wiped the spittle off his cheek and looked at the liquid on his fingers in disbelief. "You bitch! Did you just spit on me?"

I reached for my can of mace, remembering too late that it was in my jacket in the bar. I backed up in the general direction of the door, glancing around as frat boy and his dickhead buddies drew closer.

"Listen, sweetheart, you're going to come back to our place and you're going to show us all a good time, okay? In the morning we'll, I don't know, take you out for breakfast or something to say thanks."

"Fuck you, asshole!" I snarled. Without taking my eyes off of them, I reached behind me for the door handle. I cursed under my breath when I felt nothing but the rough brick wall of the bar. Where was the goddamn door?

With surprising speed, frat boy lunged for me. I opened my mouth to scream and he clamped a hard hand over my mouth. "Don't do that, sweetheart. We just want to -"

He was ripped violently away from me and I pressed my body against the wall as he was thrown to the ground. He hit the pavement with a loud thud and cursed loudly.

"I don't believe the lady is interested, little boy." Cash towered over him with his hands folded neatly behind his back.

I stared at him in relief. I think this might have been the first time I had seen Cash standing up close and I was shocked by just how large he was. My small frame was dwarfed by his and his hands were twice the size of mine.

The frat boy stumbled to his feet with his hands clenched into fists and backed up until he was standing with his buddies.

"Get out of here, man. This doesn't concern you." He tried to sound tough but even I could see the way he was trembling.

"Oh, I think it does," Cash replied mildly. "You and your little friends get in your car and get the fuck out of here."

Frat boy glanced at his friends. They nodded and he grinned at Cash. "There's four of us and only one of you. You're outnumbered, asshole."

Cash didn't reply. I was standing frozen against the wall, my heart beating too fast in my chest and my mouth tasting like frat boy and cigarettes.

"You know what they say, don't you?" Frat boy sneered. "The bigger they are, the harder they fall."

"Why don't you stop running your mouth and bring it then, little boy," Cash said quietly.

The frat boys ran forward, and I watched flabbergasted as Cash kicked the shit out of them.

ॐ ∽

"You okay?" Cash's deep voice washed over me, and I looked away from where the frat boys were lying in a crumpled heap on the cold pavement.

"I – uh, thank you?" I whispered, staring up at

him. He wasn't even breathing hard as he zipped up his leather jacket against the cold.

"No problem." He held his hand out to me. "Let's get out of here."

I hesitated. "My stuff is in the bar. My coat and my apartment keys."

"You won't need them tonight. Let's go, Del."

I was reaching for his hand before my name had even left his mouth. He led me past the moaning frat boys and toward his motorcycle. He swung his leg over it. The line of his thigh in his tight jeans made my mouth water as he beckoned to me.

"Climb on."

I nodded but before I could climb on behind him, he held out his hand. "Wait." He took his jacket off and bundled me into it. I was grateful for its warmth. My t-shirt was thin, and the air was cold.

"You're going to freeze to death," I said.

He shrugged. "I'll be fine."

He patted the seat behind him, and I hiked up my short skirt until it was just below my ass and swung into the seat. I pushed forward, my crotch jammed firmly against him and my hands linked tightly around his waist. He started the motorcycle and I jumped at the loud roar.

"Ready?" He shouted over the engine.

"Yes!" I shouted back. He lifted the kickstand, the motorcycle swayed, and I squeezed my arms around him as he tore off down the street.

∽ ∾

About the Author

Ramona Gray is a Canadian romance author. She currently lives in Alberta with her awesome husband and her mutant Chihuahua. She's addicted to home improvement shows, good coffee, and reading and writing about the steamier moments in life.

If you would like more information about Ramona, please visit her at:

www.ramonagray.ca

Books by Ramona Gray

Individual Books

The Escort
Saving Jax
The Assistant
One Night
Sharing Del
Filthy Appeal
Forbidden Bliss

Working Men Series

The Working Men Series Books 1 – 3
(The Mechanic, The Carpenter, The Bartender)
The Working Men Series Books 4 – 6
(The Welder, The Electrician, The Landscaper)
The Working Men Series Books 7 – 9
(The Firefighter, The Cop, The Paramedic)

Undeniable Series

Undeniably His
Undeniably Hers
Undeniably Theirs

Shadow Securities Series

Dead of Night
Edge of Night

Other World Series

Printed in Great Britain
by Amazon

38950645R00149